.45-CALIBER PERFUME

Also by Leo W. Banks
Double Wide
Champagne Cowboys

.45-CALIBER PERFUME

LEO W. BANKS

BOOKS

ISBN-13: 978-1-954841-49-9

Published by
Brash Books
PO Box 8212
Calabasas, CA 91372
www.brash-books.com

CHAPTER ONE

Henry Belmont put his feet on the corner of the desk and the phone to his ear. "Jack, I understand, I do. But I need to say something here and I want you to listen careful, all right? Money is the only thing."

"I know the way this works. You don't think I know?"

"Money will decide this. If it was something else, we'd be talking about something else."

The desk was huge, made of walnut, its legs carved into lions' paws. On the shelf behind it hung a photo of Henry smiling on one side, his wife, Barbara, on the other, and in the middle the president of the United States.

Next to it was a shot of a young Henry in his football uniform, kneeling, helmet on the ground beside him. He looked like the photo in a new wallet. Cool gray eyes, a movie-star jaw. His middle name was Vincent. Somebody in the media called him Vin the Chin and the nickname stuck.

"I'll do the best I can for you, Henry. But you're looking good, far as I can tell. Are you expecting a change of fortune? A sudden disaster, you know, in your numbers?"

"I can't help you, you don't help me. See what I'm saying?"

"That's bullshit. I'm surprised at you, Henry. I'm not doing my part? I haven't helped you all your life? With various situations?"

"You're surprised. Is that what you're saying? Christ."

"How long we known each other, and you say that to me. Maybe I'll drop the figure. Bring it down a little, a tax for listening to your bullshit. A bullshit tax."

"Jack, Jack."

"Screw you, my friend."

"This is the United States Senate. It takes money to beat an incumbent."

"I'm not helping you? Answer me. I'm not helping?"

"When I win, I'll be helping you. But I don't win, what happens then? You got no leverage on anything. You're just another guy on the phone wanting something and nobody's listening." Henry made his voice sound pathetic. "'Hello, anybody out there?' 'Sorry, nobody cares.' In other words, you're done for, kaput. That last one you can look up."

"You look it up. I came from nothing."

The city traffic roared outside the office window. Henry's ear was hot. He switched the phone to the other side, crooking it against his tilted head as he fingered a rubber band.

"I know you've been down broke street before, Jack. We both have."

"Rode the bus 'til I was twenty. Couldn't afford a car. I remember those days. Hitching rides. I'm never taking the bus again."

"Good. Now, calm down and let's understand each other."

"I have a figure in mind, what I'm willing to hand over."

"More. That's the only number I wanna hear from you."

"When it comes to money, I notice that's everybody's favorite. You don't even know what it is."

"I got staff to pay, the TV buys. Jesus, the TV buys are killing us. It's not even the money, it's finding a slot. They buy up all the best slots. And the locals in these towns, they all got a hand sticking out. More. That's the word they give me and that's my word for you."

"What guarantees do I get, Henry? My project. The silver ponytails are up my butt every day and more delays will kill me. Soon as the land swap gets approved, we can bring in the dozers. But I need that approval."

"A cinch. When I win. Get me? I know all the levers to pull."

"I have to trust you, right? Good thing I love you, Henry. You're a pain in the ass, but I always knew you'd make it. Now it's my turn and I want you to remember that. I'll have something ready tomorrow."

"Tomorrow? I sent Mary over there an hour ago. I need it today."

"Yeah, and I sent her back. It isn't ready."

"What do you mean it isn't ready? It's money, Jack. Cash in a sack. We're not talking about a soufflé here."

Mary Rose Cleary stepped into Henry Belmont's office. She had perfect skin, a wide mouth, and lovely green eyes. She was thin but everything fit together nicely. She had thick auburn hair, long, and a crooked nose. She wore a blue dress with a white collar.

"Here she is now."

Mary gave Henry a frustrated face and held her hands up to show they were empty. "Sorry it took so long. The traffic was murder."

"Tell Mary hello for me."

"You just saw her, Jack, like a minute ago."

"Yeah, sure. But, you know, I'm a thoughtful guy."

"Hold on. What am I looking at here? You have something creepy in mind? Some dirty business with my employee? I'm not sure I like that."

"She has a way about her. When that girl walks. Have you noticed?"

"When she walks?"

"She's kind of pretty, but not too much. She's so shy. It makes you wonder what's behind it, the situation behind it."

"I can answer that. Nothing."

Mary spread her hands to ask what was up. Henry covered the mouthpiece. "Maker's, two ice." She went into the utility room.

"She's like a work of art that you look at and you like it, but you don't have any idea why. If I can say that."

"Yeah, you can say it. It's stupid, but you can say anything you like. Just remember the word, Jack. More."

"I can go as high as five thousand."

"Tomorrow."

Henry Belmont hung up the phone. Mary handed him his drink. "What was that about?"

"These conversations are going to kill me." Henry swung his legs around and leaned forward, rubbing his neck. "I feel exhausted after."

He sipped and rubbed some more. "That's three today and more coming. Good thing the basic pitch is the same. What I got to remember is what they want, because every one of 'em wants something different. That and names. Names I mix up. Not Jack's. Jack and me, we kicked cans together. These other guys, call one of them the wrong name, and all of a sudden, I'm dancing. Doing the bossa nova."

"I like to dance." Mary turned her hip and smiled.

Henry didn't smile back. He stared, his eyes never meeting hers. "Jack Winston thinks you're shy."

"Sometimes I am. Sometimes all I want to do is dance. With you, Henry."

"Is that so." He stood and closed the door and locked it. He took off his jacket and stuck it on the hook and undressed.

"Turn off the light, baby."

Henry flipped off the overhead light. The office went dark, but for the late afternoon light at the window that framed Mary Rose Cleary. She wiggled out of her dress and grabbed Henry and pulled him down on top of her on the couch under the window.

Her raised right leg banged over and over against the blinds.

4

When they were done, Henry hurried to put his clothes back on.

"I gotta go. I'm meeting people at that place over there, the waitresses, they dress like cowgirls. What's that place, the white hats? What's it called?"

"What's the hurry, sweetheart? We could talk."

"The hurry is I got a meeting. What took you so long?"

"Traffic. I told you."

"He treats you good, doesn't he? Jack Winston. Treats you pretty good?"

"Oh, God. Is that what you're thinking? Please don't be jealous. Jack Winston? He's nothing like you, Henry."

"Really? Tell me how I am. I don't know myself, so enlighten me."

"You've got style."

"I'm no sucker, okay?"

"It's the silliest thing I ever heard. Me and Jack? All I did was walk in and walk out two minutes later."

"Jack tells me tomorrow. We'll see." Henry sipped his Maker's. "Play me and we got trouble, that's all I'm saying."

"Don't be mad. I love you. I do. In my heart."

Henry paid no attention. He was staring at his phone.

"Did you hear me?"

"I'm right here. You talk like I'm overseas. Go ahead and put your clothes back on."

"Leave the light off until I'm done." Mary dressed quickly in the dark.

"We've got an important speech tomorrow. Do yourself up nice. That red dress with the flowers on it. That one gets them going. I want everything just right."

"Everything will be perfect, Henry. I promise." She hopped up on her toes and kissed him on the cheek. "I don't like it when you get mad at me."

Henry never took his eyes off the phone.

After Henry left, Mary drove home. She lived in a ranch-style house in a tired old neighborhood. When she stepped inside, her stepmother, Dorothy, called to her from the kitchen.

"Be right there, Doe."

"Right now! I need my dinner now!"

Mary went into her bedroom, shut the door, and leaned her back against it. She closed her eyes. She felt weak in the legs and her breathing was shallow.

Don't you cry. Don't you dare cry, Mary Cleary.

Dorothy called again, louder.

"Just a moment, Doe!"

Mary went into the bathroom and looked in the mirror. Her cheeks were gray and her eyes red. She looked like something that had been run over on the street. She turned away quickly. She didn't want to see those eyes looking back at her, not now, not with her conversation with Henry looping through her head.

She heard every word again and thought of things she should've said and cursed herself for not saying them.

"Where are you, Mary?" That voice shot straight up Mary's spine. "I've been alone all day. I need my medicine!"

Please, shut up! Please, please, please!

Mary used a washcloth and warm water on her face. She was careful not to look at herself in the mirror. She toweled off and sat on the edge of her bed to steady herself. The cat walked between her legs.

"Little Muffin, there you are. I've needed you today. Come see me, sweetie." Mary swept the animal up, cuddling it against her neck. "It's going to be all right, Little Muffin. Henry loves me. He does. I know you don't believe me, but it's true. You'll see."

CHAPTER TWO

Mary got up before sunrise and went to Dorothy's bedroom to check on her. The wheelchair was beside the bed and she was spread-eagle on her back on the mattress. There was a collection of pill bottles on the night table and balled-up tissues on the floor.

Over the bed hung a photograph of Dorothy dressed in her old Salvation Army uniform.

In the kitchen, Mary made a cup of green tea and sat in the backyard. The birds sang as the sun broke. With a yellow legal pad in her lap, she watched the sky redden and tried to write her poetry.

Morning was the only tolerable time in the desert in August, before the sun rose and became a club that beat on you until your brain shut down. She struggled to get something on the page before the heat, but nothing came.

Ever since the job and Henry, she was empty.

After breakfast, Mary spent the morning working in her room, and just before noon she put on the red dress, hopped in her car, and headed to the rally.

She wasn't good at directions, but whenever she went downtown, she remembered the presidents and the Hotel San Carlos. Built early in the twentieth century, it was a boxy stone building with a long neon sign hanging off the side

She followed Central Avenue past Jackson, Madison, Jefferson, Washington, and Adams. When she saw the San Carlos up ahead, she knew the next president was Monroe. She turned there and drove down to the Phoenix Convention Center and found the right auditorium.

The seats were packed and the crowd buzzing. Backstage, Henry snapped his fingers and paced. He was tall and had wide shoulders, and his black hair showed the first wisps of silver at the ears.

Out behind the microphone, the emcee was winding up the room before making his introduction. "I can't tell you how very excited we are ..."

Henry peeked around the curtain. "Last week I had the ones with the funny hats. Who was that again?"

"The Shriners. Don't you remember? The tassels, the fez?" Mary showed him a picture on her phone.

"Yeah, yeah, I remember now. This bunch here, this is Local 380, right? Do I like these people?"

"Of course you do, silly," She patted his arm. "Henry, you've done this a million times."

"I don't know why I get so nervous."

"It's going to be just fine. You're exceptionally good at this."

"Once I get started. Once I get rolling. But beforehand—"

"You have a gift. You know how to connect with people."

"I do, don't I. I'll be all right. A million times, like you said."

Henry put his hand flat against his chest and stretched his neck. He wore a cornflower-blue sport coat, unbuttoned, over a lime-green shirt. The slide on his bola tie was a silver longhorn steer.

His hobby was bola ties. He had an extensive collection of every kind and design. He wore them to show that he understood old Arizona, the time before air-conditioning.

"Okay, Mary, here we go. Showtime. How do I look? Pretty good?"

"Pretty good."

"That's it, pretty good?"

"I promise they'll love you, Henry. You'll own this room. Go on, now."

Once Henry Belmont stepped out from behind the curtain, everything changed for him. The crowd hit him like a drug. He could feel it racing through him. He had big feet and a long, confident stride. He walked like he was marching, arms swinging, head pushed forward.

He gripped the podium with both hands and lowered his head slightly as if humbled. Twice he raised his hands to quiet the crowd. Their applause already had been fading, and his action had the calculated effect of keeping the clapping going.

"I only wish my late mother could be here. Dad died early, rest his soul, and she raised me up herself, and there were times, well, by golly, let me just say it this way—we weren't ever sure about tomorrow.

"That's why I'm running for the United States Senate. Tomorrow. I want to help the people of this state rise up and seize tomorrow the same way I did. When I was a teenager, I begged and pleaded and finally got a shovel job, my first job. I worked and worked. Nobody outworked me. Moved to Arizona, saw opportunity, and seized it. Started my own residential construction business. That's not easy. But I've worked and built it up. From the ground."

He paused. "That's my story, a true American story."

Another pause, this one longer. "Tomorrow."

Henry had spent a lot of time practicing in front of the mirror. That humble look in particular took a lot of work, getting the expression just right.

He studied recordings of his speeches, learned how to start slowly and build momentum. He listened over and over and practiced out loud. He'd learned to read crowds, knew when to pick it up and slow it down.

His timing was impeccable. At the end he talked money.

"You think you've been forgotten, don't you? Well, you haven't. Henry Belmont doesn't forget, and we've developed a unique way for the little guy to make his voice heard. Now, some people think it's undignified, our little technique here, but we don't. Frankly, we think it's a special way of connecting me to you.

"In just a moment, my trusted assistant will walk among you with a hat to take donations. That's right, in a hat, the old-fashioned way.

"Why do we do that? Because the money you give is a direct link between you and me. Your hands touched it and mine will, too, and that means a lot to me. It brings us together, and if we're going to move this country forward, we have to be together. Am I right?"

Scattered applause and hooting.

"Now, with all the taxes you pay, you might wonder what we do with this extra money. I'll tell you. We hand it out to the lost souls you see out on the sidewalks, on street corners, those sad camps everywhere, in our parks, downtown.

"You drive by and think, that's awful. What can I do? This is what you can do. Drop a quarter or a dollar into the hat and join me, won't you? Our goal every time is to fill the hat, and today I can see it's a big one."

Henry pointed. "Take a gander back there and see for yourself."

The audience turned, murmuring, straining to see.

Mary stood by the rear doors wearing the red flowered dress and a black straw crochet-style cowboy hat. The crown was high and center-dented with a turquoise-studded band around it. The side brims were curled up and the front brim pulled low over her eyes, highlighting their striking green.

She had the cyclone string tight under her chin, framing her face. A white feather dangled off the back.

"Look who's graced us with her presence. It's the lovely Miss Mary. Let's give her a good ol' Arizona welcome."

To the cheers of the crowd, Mary walked down the center aisle, waving from one side to the other. The rising energy filled her up, and her normal reserve melted away. With Henry Belmont urging her on, she turned to face the crowd, threw her arms in the air, and bent her knee like a schoolgirl.

The crowd clapped and whistled. Mary smiled, stuck two fingers in her mouth and whistled back. That made them clap louder.

"I see Miss Mary's a bronco buster today. That's part of the fun for me. I never know what kind of gal I'll get. She brings a different hat every time. Will she be a vaquero? A wrangler? A rodeo queen?"

His voice rose on each possibility.

"I don't know until she appears. And there she goes!"

Mary took off the hat, fluffed out her hair, and began moving up and down the aisles collecting donations. Henry brought his voice back down. He looked at the ceiling, scrunched up his face, and breathed in and out audibly, a signal for the audience to get ready because he was about to say something important.

"I'd never ask you to give one cent more than you can. That's because Henry Belmont knows you, the working men and women of this country. He knows your fight. I understand what you go through to put food on the table, go to the doctor, and buy clothes for the little ones."

Mary held the hat over her head as she squeezed through the rows. She had a pure smile that included her eyes, and she knew how to use her hips. Some donors had to reach up. Some stood on their toes and a few climbed on chairs.

"My motto is whatever you can, whatever you feel comfortable giving. A buck, five bucks. If you give the most you can, I'll know it comes straight from the heart. A dollar from a working-man means more to me than a grand from some arse-you-know-what in a Mercedes."

The crowd roared with laughter. Henry made a face and put his palm over his mouth like a child who'd said something fresh.

"I gotta watch my tongue, but dang it, sometimes the unfairness in this world, the injustice, I can't look on and not do something. I won't stay quiet!"

Someone in the crowd shouted, "Vin the Chin will never stay quiet!"

A different voice: "We hear you, Mr. Belmont!"

Henry cupped his hand behind his ear. "What's that?"

"You're our man, Vin the Chin!"

"I'm sorry. All those years working construction, wrangling a jackhammer, why, my ears don't work so good. Tell me again, who's your man?"

"Vin the Chin!"

Henry raised his jaw and stuck it out until it practically hit the ceiling. That was his signature move. "One more time!"

"Vin the Chin! Vin the Chin!"

The floor shook. You could feel the vibration under your feet. The dollar bills fell like rain into Mary's hat.

Henry smiled a big one. "Darn right! I hear you!"

The crowd kept cheering and stomping. "Vin the Chin! Vin the Chin!"

Afterward, backstage, Mary was so jazzed she couldn't stand still. Press secretary Monica Gomez was there, too, cool as usual, businesslike, studying her tablet. She was chubby and wore a blue pantsuit. "You okay, Henry? That was good work. I think we earned some votes out there."

"Thanks, Mon."

"We got that meeting later, remember. I'll go talk to the dogs." That was what Gomez called the press. She left.

Henry was sitting on a folding chair, jacket off, sleeves rolled up, mopping his forehead with a hanky. "She's right. That was a helluva good show. We hit a home run, Barb."

Barbara Belmont stood beside him looking bored. "Eh." She wiggled her hand. "Maybe a ground-ball double."

"No, no, no. I was on fire. Didn't you see me out there? Are you blind?"

Barbara had been a real beauty in her youth. But the years had hardened her face. Her skin was tight, the lips Botox full and painted a bright red. Her eyes were a washed-out amber. Without light. Nightclub eyes.

Her natural hair color was lost to history now, but today it was strawberry blond, shoulder-length, layered and styled to look messy. No matter what she wore, her figure stood out, and when she entered a room, chin up, striding, there was always a murmur, and it came as much from women as from men.

She pointed at Mary. "You don't give this one enough credit, Henry."

"Huh? Who?"

"Your girl here, your campaign manager. Hello? Remember her?"

"Oh, yeah. We work good together."

"I'm sure you do."

Mary bounced from foot to foot, slightly breathless, her face florid.

Hands on hips, Barbara studied her up and down and back again. "The good Lord didn't give you much, but you know how to use what you got."

"Me? Oh, I wouldn't say that, Mrs. Belmont."

"You almost got a stampede going out there. That hat dance you do."

"It's nothing special. It's just men, the way they are."

"Some of the women, too. I know you saw. They were up on their feet."

"Really, I didn't notice."

"Uh-huh."

CHAPTER THREE

Phoenix is a freeway city. Cussing at the traffic on the freeways is the only thing everyone has in common. That and getting lost in IKEA.

It's a boulevard town, too, long stretches of broad boulevards with palm trees lining the way, traffic lights every half mile and fast-food restaurants and banks on just about every corner, and in between, a long string of storefronts for places like TGI Fridays, Target, and Best Buy.

The Belmont campaign had offices on the ground floor of a glass-and-brick office building on one of those boulevards, Thomas Road east of downtown. Henry, Mary, and Barbara got there late that afternoon.

The room was large, the carpet white. There were two small utility rooms off the office. In the first one Henry kept office supplies and his extensive collection of premium liquors. The second room, a tiny bathroom, had a dartboard hanging on the door.

Mary counted the cash from the hat. It totaled $1,876. The take usually ran around $1,500, so that was a good day.

"You got the right hat, Mary. I'm telling you, the hat's key. When you choose the right one, we really clean up, and that was a corker."

Henry gathered the bills into a stack and fastened them with a rubber band. He fanned the stack under his nose. "Nothing smells like money. Ever notice that? Musty. Is that the word? Like it came out of a box in the crawl space." He gave the stack another whiff. "Damn, I love that smell."

"Better count it again, Henry. Make sure I didn't make a mistake."

"You don't make mistakes. That's why I hired you three years outta college."

"Are you saying I'm smart? That you couldn't get by without me?"

Barbara rolled her eyes. "Is that what you think, sugar?"

"I'm teasing Mr. Belmont. With these campaign days being so long and all, we like to keep things light."

"He's saying he can't count. There's a friggin' difference."

"Barbara."

"Henry."

They traded annoyed looks.

Henry handed the money to Mary, changed his mind, pulled it back, and peeled off several bills and stuffed them in his pocket.

"I need to get gas on the way home." He snapped the rubber band back on. "Those guys sleeping outside the library, they need to eat. Buy McDonald's for them and make sure everybody knows where it came from. Make a fuss about it. You know how to do this." He handed the stack to Mary.

"Sure thing, Henry. On the way home. Big Macs and Cokes all the way around."

"Oh, and make sure there's plenty of cash left over to bring to the Boys Home around the corner. Tell Sherry it's from Henry. She's a top-notch gal, running that place over there by herself. I don't know how she does it. She needs all the help she can get."

Sherry Waterman was director of the Boys Home. When Henry Belmont played football at Texas, she was one of the cheerleaders. They'd dated through all four years and were together on the debate team as well.

The phone rang. Henry spotted the number. "Jack Winston. Say howdy to Jackie boy." He punched in but didn't say hello. Nobody says hello to old friends. You just start up. "I hope you're calling with good news."

"Your package is ready."

"I'll send Mary over. It's about time, by the way."

"That should keep your numbers up for a while."

"Polls go up and down all the time. I don't trust 'em. Tomorrow I could be underwater. More, Jack."

Henry hung up. "Five grand. What a piker. I'm getting three times that today alone, these phone calls I'm making, and he's my best friend. But that's Jack Winston for you. You're on tap, Mary, Jack's office."

"I'll call Fat Frankie and set up the deposit."

"Hold on." Barbara Belmont scowled at the mention of Frankie's name. "I can't believe you use that guy, Henry."

"Frankie? Frankie's solid, Frankie's good."

"You sure about that?"

"Ever hear the name Chino Carrasco?"

"Yeah, the drug guy, the one the feds tried to nail. Dicked it up so bad he walked."

"Frankie washes money for Chino and skims some off for himself. Nobody knows that, but I happen to know it, and never mind how. And Frankie knows I know. In my world they call that leverage."

Henry told Mary to make the call. They'd done this many times before, and it was quick. She arranged to pick up Frankie at his restaurant at 4:00 p.m. and drive him to the bank.

On her way out the door Henry stopped her. "Been meaning to tell you. Get me a box of cigars. Can you get me a box of Cohibas? You know what they are, don't you?"

"Yes, illegal. Aren't they Cuban cigars?"

"Somebody in the Valley has to have a box of them or knows how we can get one."

"For election night? It's not good to be planning your party too soon. You'll jinx it."

"Just do it, okay?"

"Cigars aren't exactly my priority right now, Henry. What about Mike?"

"Mary, crissakes, show some initiative. I need my people to have initiative."

She exhaled in frustration. "I'll make some calls."

"You do that. Send Monica and Mike in on your way out."

Mary gathered her things and the money, said good night, and went out. Monica came in with political director Mike Papadopoulos. He was twenty-seven, didn't stand much over five foot five, had thick black eyebrows.

Scary smart, he talked a lot, and rapid fire. "We need to change how we talk about taxes, Henry. So people can relate. Tell stories about real families, names and all. Monica's on board."

The two of them stood in front of Henry's desk. Papadopoulos could barely see over it.

"Mike's right. I jotted some ideas." Monica handed him a piece of paper.

Henry ignored it, got up, and fixed himself a drink in Fort Recovery, what he called his supply room. Horse Soldier bourbon. He sipped his drink and put the glass down on his desk.

"All right, what's this story thing about?"

Monica and Mike talked as Henry threw darts, his habit when he and his staff were thinking things over. They talked for ten minutes. Henry nodded in agreement throughout and sent them away. He refreshed his drink and went back to throwing darts.

Barbara sighed as if relieved. "Listening to those two all day, I'd stick my head in the oven. Or theirs." She was sitting on the couch drinking an Old Forester rye. The bracelets over both wrists jangled when she moved. A shaman made less noise. Her fingernails were long, glossy, and red.

Watching Henry, his shoulders, his long legs, she took a swallow, kicked off her shoes, and crossed her legs lazily, inching her skirt up. "Whaddya say, wanna recreate?" She patted the cushion next to her. "Get some exercise after a long day."

"Ah, yeah, no. I got a lot on my mind."

"You're no fun." Barbara looked into her glass but didn't drink. Something distracted her. She stared for a second and her face went up and her nostrils flared.

"Dior."

"What door?"

"Christian Dior. The perfume I'm getting off this couch."

"You must be a tick hound." Henry threw a dart. "All I get is dust."

Barbara had had her suspicions about Mary and Henry. The scent from the couch left no doubt. That was the brand Mary wore—J'Adore by Christian Dior.

"Are you sure it's smart to use that girl as a courier?"

"She doesn't talk too much. I trust her."

"All that cash she's carrying around, you better."

Henry threw two more darts, emptying his hand. He picked up his bourbon and drained the glass and went into Fort Recovery and poured more. "Know what she does nights? Mary?"

He used tongs to drop two ice cubes into his glass. He took a long sip as he walked back into the office. The booze put a rasp in his voice.

"Takes care of her stepmother. Her stepmother's got something wrong with her, some shit going on. Uses a wheelchair. I don't know, rolls around. Mary cooks her supper every night, cleans her up, puts her to bed."

He waved the glass in the air. "I don't worry about somebody like that. If you know anything about people, Mary's fine."

"The Frankie thing worries me, Henry."

"We talked about this. The office is out, the house is out, so where? A bank is the only safe place and I'm sure as hell not going to put money in my name or Mary's or yours. Somebody comes poking around, I'm sunk. Frankie's perfect."

"If he's dumb enough to steal from a killer like Chino Carrasco, why wouldn't he steal from you?"

Henry reached into his pocket and pulled out a penny. "See this? Guess who it is on there? That ain't Abe Lincoln, that's Frankie Santiago." He went back to throwing darts, leaning forward, tongue sticking out between his teeth. "Anytime I want, I can reach into my pocket and there's Fat Frankie. He's like an old penny."

"Pennies ain't worth much."

"This one's worth a fortune. If I need fast cash, I name the amount and old Abe delivers."

"Okay, so Mary doesn't go into the bank, right? That's the way you two work it? Because you don't want her on camera? Fine. So Frankie goes in alone and snatches a few bucks outta that pouch every time. Right? It adds up."

"Carrasco's got the real money. Why bother with me?"

"Since when is enough, enough? They call it greed. You'd never know, Henry. You don't keep track. What about the deposit slips?"

"Mary checks them. Frankie keeps them, but Mary checks them first. On my orders. We got it all worked out. Don't worry."

"Running the business now, being the hot-shot general manager, know what I think when one of my people says 'Don't worry?' I think, 'Oh, shit.'"

"You want me to keep receipts? Maybe I should write the numbers in a notebook? When the feds come poking around, I can go, 'Sure, here it is, all spelled out nice for you.' I wouldn't look so good in paper slippers."

"I'm just telling you, you play it too loose."

Henry pointed to the dartboard. "See that? Bull's-eye. What luck. No, it's not luck, I'm good. I'm putting on a show here. Are you paying attention?"

"You have to keep track."

"Drop it, will you."

"Loose as a goose, Henry. Loose as a goose."

"Stop saying that."

"I don't trust that sweet little girl either."

"Mary? You're crazy."

CHAPTER FOUR

It was a breezy day. The sun hid behind a low-hanging haze the color of the desert.

Mary drove on Jefferson Street two blocks past the copper-domed state capitol building to El Toreador, the first restaurant Frankie Santiago opened in the city. On the roof stood a big neon matador all decked out in red and black.

He was waving a red cape. At night, drivers could see his blinking mustache for miles.

The neighborhood around it was seedy. The houses had bars on the windows and junk cars outside, and if you were walking along the sidewalk, you'd cross the street to avoid the groups of bug-eyed men huddled around.

That didn't bother Frankie's regulars. Most were state representatives and senators and lobbyists and all the others who cling to the wheel of power. They liked to have meetings in the private room in back, and Frankie saw to them personally. Some of the state people were bug-eyed, too.

Frankie was waiting on the sidewalk, looking up and down the street, an empty pouch in his hand. Mary beeped. He saw the car and waved. The suspension on it squealed when he plopped onto the seat.

"Thought I was gonna die out there. I've got serious pits."

"Don't do that."

"You look lovely this afternoon, Mary."

"Thank you, thank you." She pulled the cash from her purse and handed it to Frankie. He put it in the pouch and zipped it up.

"What's the number for today?"

"Four thousand." Mary had taken her cut.

"That's it? Is Henry sliding?"

"Are you kidding? The money's pouring in. Mr. Belmont's doing just fine, don't you worry. Our data models look good."

Frankie's round face gleamed with sweat. He had brown eyes and stubby rivet fingers. He didn't need a shave right then, but he would in an hour. He wore a maroon sport shirt with Arizona State University's golden pitchforks on the chest. When he smiled, his teeth were invisible under a push-broom mustache.

"I don't know from data models and don't care. Mary, I think about you all the time."

"You do? Whatever for?" She liked this part. It was so easy.

"What for, that's a good one. You know what for. Let's get together and have a party, just me and you."

"Like a date?"

"Not like a date, a date. An official *date* date."

She had driven east past the capitol and got onto Central Avenue north. "What about your wife? You've been married forever, right?"

"I thought you knew, she took off."

"Don't even! I had no idea."

"Yeah, yeah. Big news, leaving on a jet plane." He started singing the song. "Had just about enough of me."

"I'm so sorry. Gee. Really."

"My charms were lost on her."

"How's that even possible?"

"That's what I said. Charms? Right? She must've had me confused with somebody else."

Mary drove along, tapping the brakes. That time of day the traffic on Central was all choked up. She was a terrible driver, always going too slow or too fast, cutting people off. She kept both hands on the wheel and her arms straight out, eyes fixed and bulging.

Cars zoomed around her on both sides, and she got mean looks. The intersection with Indian School Road was coming up.

"No, seriously, she said I gained too much weight. She couldn't be around me anymore because I got fat. You believe that?"

"Are you kidding me?"

"I'm not making it up. You break one chair."

"That's no reason to leave somebody. That's cruel. Besides, you have yummy food."

"Best in the Valley. Got a plaque from those guys at that weekly, that rag."

"Everybody loves your dishes. I couldn't be around it all day without sampling this and that."

"After all these years together, she quit liking me. That was the whole thing of it, and you know what?"

"That's too bad."

"I don't care. When she took off, felt like I got parole."

"Frankie, you don't mean that. You miss her, I'm sure."

"Listen, up in Cave Creek, I got a place nobody knows about."

"Reeeally." She knew what was coming.

"Let's you and me head up there for a rendezvous. Big house, hot tub, the whole sexy inventory."

"Aren't you the playboy? I don't know."

"Get this. I got a TV in the bathroom. I'm not fooling, it's in the flipping can. Right up on the wall."

"That's not a selling point, Frankie. I hate to tell you, not to a proper lady."

"It's my special getaway. You gotta see it."

Mary knew exactly how he'd paid for it, too. "I don't know. We're so busy with the campaign right now, moving ahead on different policy initiatives."

She flipped on her blinker to turn onto Indian School.

"Then, you need a break, don't you? All this work."

"Let's say I might call you sometime in the future. Might, might. Okay, Frankie?" She held up a cautioning finger. "That's not a promise."

"How about a kiss to tide me over? Give you something to dream about."

He leaned over. She put out her hand to hold him back.

"Frankie, stop. I'm trying to drive. This is hard enough for me without somebody trying to kiss me."

"I'm a desperate man, Mary."

"You can be desperate some other time. Do you see this traffic?"

"I'm a man on a mission." He gave a laugh that came from deep down, a loud *har, har, har.* He calmed himself, sighing long. He sat with his palms on his knees. "Oh, me. What can you do?"

"You're terrible."

Frankie owned three successful restaurants. The others were in Mesa and Scottsdale, and they raked it in every day. Depositing frequent loads of cash in different accounts was normal business for him. They were his daily receipts.

Do it right and nobody asks questions. No eyebrows go up.

But you had to be careful. There are plenty of laws against washing money and lots of law enforcement looking around. Be disciplined, follow the rules. Keep the deposits in the same range every day. No big jumps.

It helped that his restaurants were popular. No wonder he handled all that cash every day. The waitstaff couldn't know anything, and it helped to seed the tip jar every day to keep them happy. Frankie was good at that.

For the politicians and the cops who came in, he made a point of taking care of them, too. Greeted them all personally.

Big handshakes, two hands. "Your table is ready. Right this way." Good old Frankie.

Once in the bank, that money was clean. There's no better way to hide money than a restaurant that handles a lot of cash every day.

The Wells Fargo branch wasn't far along on Indian School. Mary turned her blue Corolla into the lot and pulled behind a minivan, near the bank's front doors but shielded from its cameras.

Sitting in her car, Barbara Belmont watched from across the street.

Frankie walked to the door, held it open for a woman exiting, gave a grand sweep of his hand like a big shot, and went inside. He was gone fifteen minutes. When he came out, arms swinging, whistling as he walked, he got back in Mary's car, breathing hard and sweating again.

"Everything go okay?"

"Same as always. You get to know the people after a while, the tellers. I like that. They're always nice to me."

He held the receipt up to Mary. Without looking at it, she waved him off. "Gosh, Frankie, you don't have to show me every time. You know I trust you." Truth was, she'd trust a Doberman with a steak bone more than Frankie Santiago.

"That makes me feel good." He stuffed the receipt in his pocket.

The two of them drove away in Mary's Corolla. Barbara didn't follow. She supposed that Mary would drop Frankie back at El Toreador and drive home. It was coming up on suppertime, and she had to feed her stepmom.

But Barbara wanted to make sure.

Wearing a ball cap and black sunglasses, she swung in behind them heading the opposite way on Central. Barbara had gotten good at tailing. With all the boyfriends she'd had over the years, she considered herself an expert.

The traffic made it easier. Plenty of places to hide and nobody was going anywhere fast. She stayed a couple of cars behind, timed the lights beautifully, and when it became clear that Mary would drop Frankie back at El Toreador, she broke off and headed for Mary's house.

CHAPTER FIVE

Barbara parked several houses down and waited. An hour passed before Mary's Corolla rolled up and turned into her driveway. Her house was on South Fourth Street near Chase Field, a faded white stucco, single story, needing a paint job.

The roof had missing tiles around an evaporative cooler box. There was a single-car garage on the left side and in front one of those rock-and-cactus lawns that start out looking good, then the weeds grow and nobody pulls them and it looks like a vacant lot.

Barbara watched with binoculars. Mary stepped out of her car wearing the black straw hat from the convention center. She threw her purse strap over her shoulder, took a few quick steps, stopped as if she'd heard or seen something, peered around, and hurried into the house.

Looking hard, Barbara spotted a white envelope sticking up from a side pocket of Mary's purse. It could've been anything, the electric bill, work papers, or a flyer from Ted's Tasty Pizza.

But Barbara figured it wasn't any of those things. First the perfume and now this. Barbara figured Mary was spinning Henry's dials with sex and stealing his money.

She had to find out for sure.

To avoid staying in one place too long, she pulled out and circled the block and parked in a different location on the street. The sun still hung up in the sky. She didn't want to make a move until darkness. She waited.

In the kitchen, as Mary fixed supper, Dorothy badgered her more than usual.

"Why were you late? You know I don't like it when you're late."

"Work."

"The older I get, the less I like being alone. Every sound I hear has me jumping."

"I came as soon as I could get away."

Dorothy reached into the side pocket on her wheelchair and pulled out a pistol. She held it in her frail hand like it weighed a hundred pounds. "If it wasn't for this, I don't know what I'd do. It keeps me calm, just knowing it's there."

"I can't believe you still have that cannon. How old is it?"

"My great-great-grandpa Horace carried it in the Civil War. Chickamauga, everywhere else, too. Tennessee, Georgia, shooting Yankees left and right. It's a Smith & Wesson Old Army revolver. Probably worth some money, too."

"Probably doesn't shoot, more like it."

You could put it to your head and find out.

Dorothy dropped the gun back into the side pocket. "By the way, when are you going to sell my Prius? How many times have I said, sell my car, sell my car? You know I can't drive anymore and it's just sitting there."

"Haven't gotten around to it."

"Well, hurry it up. I need a new TV, a big screen would be nice. One of those really big ones so I can look right up people's noses." She laughed. Her teeth were worn and spotted. "I thought you didn't like having to park in the driveway. Out in the open like that."

"I don't. It's hot."

"Well, sell my car and go ahead and park in the garage. You won't have to get into a hot car. See? We both get what we want. And paint the house. You were supposed to paint the house, remember, and that's not done either."

"I have everything in the garage, the paint and everything. I just haven't gotten time off."

"It's looking shabby, don't you think?"

"It's been a long day, Doe."

"My birthday's coming up, you know. A TV would be a very nice present."

Out on the street, Barbara stepped out of her car and walked up the sidewalk. She slipped into the shadows at the side of the house and around to the Arizona room in back. It was screened from the waist up, the door unlocked.

As quietly as she could, Barbara sneaked inside and planted herself under the open window separating the porch from the kitchen. Certain she hadn't been detected, she gripped the sill and rose to look.

She saw Mary and Dorothy sitting at the table, eating silently. A long time passed with no words between them, only a deep quiet broken by the excruciating clank of silverware on plates.

Watching, Barbara could feel the tension. After a while, Dorothy started up again.

"Are there any interesting men at your work? That you could get involved with."

"I don't know, maybe. There might be one."

"By interesting I mean a man of means. We need help around here and you're not doing enough."

"Things will change, Doe. I promise. I'm getting to where I can buy a lot of the things you want."

"It's not that I haven't waited. Tell me about this man."

"Nothing's definite, but things are happening."

"That sounds interesting. The workplace isn't just for work, no matter what they say these days. Now I really want to know."

"He's older and so handsome, my word."

"Well, all right. That's what I like to hear. Does he wear a pocket hanky? Regis had nice pocket hankies. Red, yellow, all colors. You can tell a man of means by his pocket hanky."

"That's on TV and somebody else dresses them. So..."

"This fellow, would I know his name? Is he a candidate for high office, by any chance?"

Looking around, Barbara could see Mary and Dorothy, the table and chairs, but not Mary's purse. She went to the window on the other side of the kitchen door and looked in at the main part of the kitchen, the oven, the refrigerator, and the counter-tops around the sink.

No purse anywhere.

She exited the Arizona room and sneaked around to the front of the house and looked through the large front window at the lighted living room. There was a couch against the wall with an easy chair beside it.

Farther across the room was a TV. *Jeopardy!* was on. The purse wasn't on top of the TV, or on the couch or the coffee table. All the other rooms were dark. Barbara went back to the Arizona room and crouched in the same place by the window, watching and listening.

"I don't want to spook it, Doe. But I might have news after the election."

"About time. What I always say, if you're alone with a man every day and can't make him notice you, it's your own fault. You can look good when you want to. You used to look cute in that hiking outfit you had, those cute shorts. Whatever happened to them?"

"Can't exactly wear them to the office, Doe."

"Does your man hike? You two could go hiking. There's a lot of romantic places in the mountains. Big lakes and things. You used to hike all the time."

"I know every trail in the Superstitions backward and for-ward. But with this job, there's no time. I'm working all the time."

"How about fixing yourself up better?"

Mary felt the rope tighten around her neck. "Can we just eat, please?"

"Makeup, some nice clothes. You never learned to put on makeup. When I was your age, why, men noticed me, I guarantee you. I could give you tips."

"Oh, boy. I'll write them down."

"I had a bell to ring, but I didn't need no bell. Men would get a look and come over. Drop in some cash and say a few words. How much is he worth, your man?"

"Dorothy. Honestly."

"What? Your father left me nothing. You know what that's like?"

"Isn't my soup wonderful tonight?"

"It's too hot for soup. Don't tell me that's wrong, Mary, I won't hear it. First your father and now you. I don't want to die poor."

"I'm going to go online and pick out a new TV for you."

"That's what I like to hear. Remember, right up their noses!" Dorothy broke up laughing.

After supper, Dorothy sat in front of the TV in the living room. Mary went down the hall to her bedroom.

When she turned on the light, Barbara sneaked off the porch and followed the glow around to the other side of the house to a slab of cement that looked like the start of a patio that hadn't been finished. French doors led into Mary's bedroom.

Barbara peered inside through a narrow crack in the curtains.

The room had a bookshelf full of hardbacks and a desk against the wall. On top were two laptops and stacks of paper. The hat Mary had worn at the speech was on the bed, the purse next to it, but the envelope wasn't in the side pocket.

She'd already put it away. But where? If she'd been stealing for any length of time, she'd have a nice bundle stashed away somewhere.

A car door slammed on the street behind Barbara, loud enough to make her jump. She pulled away from the doors, listening. She heard no voices, only faint descending footsteps, and when the footsteps died and the street fell silent, she peered into the bedroom again.

Mary pulled her dress off over her head and dropped it on the bed. She reached back and unhooked her bra and flung it on top of the dress. She curled one arm behind her and bent her torso back to stretch, then scratched underneath her breasts as she went into the bathroom, out of Barbara's view.

She returned with her hair up wearing a robe. It was open, and from the side, Barbara could see Mary's bare leg as she walked.

Mary grabbed the hat off the bed, put it on, and looked at herself in the mirror above the dresser. She tipped her head one way and the other. She fingered the brim back to show more of her face and smiled at herself. She liked that look, the hair falling across her forehead.

Lighthearted, daring, ready for anything.

This is the look I need to show Henry.

She gave herself a tip of the hat, sat at the desk, opened one of the laptops, and started typing. A screen of TVs popped up. Mary scrolled. After a few minutes of staring at the screen, she reached into the center drawer, took out a key, and unlocked the bottom right-hand drawer.

She opened it and stared into it. She looked for a long time before going back to scrolling. A few minutes later, she looked again, and then again, staring longer each time.

Another car door slammed out on South Fourth Street, and there were voices close by. Barbara waited until all the sounds stopped and the people had gone on their way.

With the night quiet again, she left her spy place at Mary's door and drove home.

CHAPTER SIX

The Belmonts lived in a sprawling multilevel mountain home in Scottsdale. Natural stone steps curled up the side of a ridge to the front door. It had a mud-and-adobe exterior and red scored-concrete floors inside. The living room had a stone fireplace with a Navajo chief's blanket on the wall above.

Barbara was asleep when Henry got home that night. She woke up when he crawled into bed, but they exchanged no words. In the morning, they traded only shouted good-byes, upstairs to downstairs, as Henry left early for the office.

As soon as she heard the front door close and Henry's Lexus pull away, she got out of bed. She liked being in the house alone. Every sound was hers and everything she did was known only to her.

She poured orange juice and carried it upstairs with her to drink while she got ready. For what Barbara had in mind, there was no need to hurry. She did her makeup and got dressed. She chose a green dress with white trim and ruffles at the shoulders. Only minor cleavage, just a taste. The dress was tight fitting and left no doubts, but it wasn't too flashy either.

The shoes took the most time. Barbara didn't scrimp when it came to shoes. She kept them in a separate walk-in closet bigger than most bedrooms. She chose tortoise-heel pumps with a pointed toe.

She finished dressing and went to the Starbucks drive-through on Scottsdale Road and Goldwater. Reggie, the cheery tattooed barista, served up her usual, a Venti iced Americano with a shot of espresso and whipped cream on top.

"Extra whipped cream, Mrs. Belmont, just how you like it."

"You're the best, Reggie."

She put her nose to the foam and sipped. She came away with a white mustache. "Ouch, that is so good. Let me get a butt going here and it'll be a perfect morning. Want one, Reggie?"

"Can't when I'm working, Mrs. Belmont. Besides, I'm trying to quit."

"What for?"

"It's bad for you, isn't it?"

"Where'd you hear that? Kids these days." She lit a cigarette, tossed him a five-dollar bill, waved good-bye, and drove off.

It was just past 7:30. Barbara knew that Mary's work mornings moved along with the precision of a clock. That meant she'd just backed the Corolla out of the driveway.

Barbara drove back to Mary's street. She parked and waited to give Mary plenty of time to get to work, and more time to make sure she hadn't forgotten something and needed to return.

Barbara had downloaded all her favorite musicals onto her phone. They were how she passed the time. Musicals made her happy. She'd picture the dancers and sing along and tap her toe and try to forget everything. Today it was *Oklahoma!*.

She smoked and sipped her drink and sang and everything was good until the heat intensified. Sometimes you can hear it building, like the faint groan of a powerful engine.

Even through the early hours, even over the storm of the air conditioner, that sound broke through. It stirred Barbara's mind and the images flooded up. She knew what was coming and sang louder to drive them off.

The wind came sweeping down the plain, all right. She pictured that waving wheat.

But nothing worked, and she saw herself, a little girl walking inside the razor-wire walls and sitting on her mother's knee in the cold green room with the guards standing by, sour, somber, stone-faced.

Dressed in a prison jumpsuit, her mother threw her arms around little Barbara and swept her off her feet, and that powerful smell—was it bleach? some industrial cleaner?—hung in the air like a noxious cloud.

Even now, sitting in the car, that smell filled Barbara's nose. Breathing faster, she opened the window to get some air.

"Welcome to my special palace. You have nothing to worry about here, my darling. These men with the badges? They take care of me. They're my friends. They do everything for me. Mommy is just fine."

She pulled little Barbara onto her lap. The grip was too tight.

Let me go. Nothing about this is right.

Some of the other visitors were crying and some shouting. Barbara wanted to run. She'd tried that before but wasn't fast enough, and everything with Steve, her mother's boyfriend, got worse after she ran.

"He'll take good care of you. He knows you're my baby, don't you, Steve?"

"I give her everything a girl could want."

When he put his hand on her shoulder, Barbara felt sick. Then came her mother's final, too-hard, smothering bleach-hug and Steve taking Barbara by the hand and leading her outside to the car, and side-watching her as he drove home.

She knew exactly what was coming.

The music still played but Barbara had stopped singing. She felt trapped. She threw open the car door to give the memory room to escape, to let the breeze carry it away.

Back to hell. Back where it came from.

She closed her eyes and ground her teeth until her jaw hurt, until she was sure it was gone, until she could breathe again, and

the pictures left her mind. With a few swipes at her hair and a
lipstick touch-up, she was ready for work, ready to do what she
did best.

She stepped out of the car and walked up the sidewalk and
knocked on Mary's front door.

"I'm sorry to disturb you. You're Dorothy, aren't you?"

"Ah, yes, I am. And you are?"

Dorothy had small, wet eyes. The skin around them made
a spider's web. She had stringy white hair with streaks of burnt
brown that looked almost orange. In the wheelchair she was
shapeless, a pile of teddy bear nightdress with her liver-spotted
hands sticking out.

She wore fuzzy white slippers. The veins around her ankles
were like blue lightning.

"I work at Mary's office and she asked me to stop by. She forgot some important work papers and it was on my way. They're
right on top of her desk in her bedroom."

"I see. You mean you'd like to go and get them?"

"If you don't mind."

Wary, Dorothy let her hand inch slowly down to the big pistol. "Why, of course. Heaven be. Down the hall, first door on the
left. You won't be long, will you? I have my morning shows."

"Not at all."

Mary had a four-poster canopy bed. Not much decoration on
the walls, only a framed Edward Hopper print of a woman in a
cloche hat sitting alone at a diner. Under Barbara's spy window,
lined up on a table against the wall, were seven white wig heads,
each topped by a Western hat from one of Henry's rallies.

She had drawn facial features on them with a black laundry
marker. The markings were expertly done. They looked like real
faces.

Barbara felt as if she were being watched. She tried not to
look back.

The dresser was opposite the bed. Nothing unusual on top. Two jewelry boxes, some perfume vials. The drawers were stuffed with the usual clothing items.

She noticed a half-moon drag mark on the carpet in front of the dresser. Barbara gripped it with both hands and swung it away from the wall and saw a square-shaped hole in the drywall filled with a sheet of plywood.

"Hello, down there!" Dorothy, shouting. "Madam, is everything all right?"

"Yes. Just fine."

"You said you wouldn't be long."

"One more moment. I'm finding just what I need."

Barbara got down on her knees, grabbed the plywood sheet at both ends, squeezed, and pulled it out. There was a small safe behind it. She'd found where Mary was keeping the money.

Now all I have to do is figure out how to get inside.

She put the plywood panel back, pushed the bureau against the wall, and moved to the desk. There was a globe on top, two black porcelain birds, a pretty photo of a stream running through a walled canyon, and a mahogany mantel clock.

The desk had seven drawers, one in the center, three on each side. She went through them individually, careful to open and close the drawers quietly. Contents normal. Paper, office supplies, bank statements. Mary had $427 in her checking account.

"Madam! You're certainly taking your time!"

"On my way." Barbara scooped some papers off the desk and rolled them up to use as cover. She had one drawer left to go, right-side bottom, the one Mary had repeatedly stared into.

Barbara found the key in the center drawer and got the big bottom one open.

Inside was a Glock pistol, the thirteen-round magazine fully loaded.

Under her breath: "Well, well. A college girl with a .45."

CHAPTER SEVEN

Barbara spent the next day at the company. She had meetings in the morning and wore a hard hat at a job site in the afternoon. But she couldn't concentrate on business. She had a big night planned.

When it got dark, she drove to Henry's office on Thomas and parked outside, waiting for Mary Rose Cleary to leave. With the AC humming, her head back against the rest, she sang along to music from *Phantom of the Opera*.

She loved that one, too. Between *Phantom* and *Oklahoma!*, it was always a close call which was better. Sometimes the winner depended on the day or her mood. She had great debates with herself about it.

She sat there for two hours. Whenever one of Henry's staffers left the building, she ducked down across the seat. Here came Papadopoulos with his tie still hitched up tight and his snappy briefcase, and a moment later Monica Gomez in her tentlike pantsuit.

Learn how to dress, girl. You look like a pie wagon in that thing.

Barbara knew how many staffers there were and she counted how many had left, until there could be only two remaining, Henry and Mary. They were caught up in another grueling night of campaign work. Barbara could tell by the thrashing of the blinds at the window.

They exited the front door together at 11:00 p.m. They were being careful. They didn't hug or kiss on the sidewalk, or say a single word, before separating and getting into their cars and driving away.

They went in the same direction on Thomas Road. Barbara slipped in behind them for a short distance before Mary turned south on Seventh Street toward her house in the old neighborhood. Henry continued east into Scottsdale.

Barbara stayed on Mary's bumper. At the first red light they came to, she pulled up behind Mary, got out, walked ahead, and tapped on her window.

Mary jumped a mile. The window came down.

"Mrs. Belmont. You—you startled me. What—what're you doing?"

"I need to ask you something."

"Here?"

"What do you plan to do with the money you're stealing from my husband?"

"The money I'm—what?" Mary looked around, stalling, the panic gathering inside her. "What're you talking about? I'm sorry, but I don't know what you're talking about."

Horns sounded behind them. First one car and then another pulled out and sped around them. One of the drivers shouted as he passed.

"I'm talking about the cash you're storing in that safe of yours."

Mary's mouth opened but nothing came out. The horns got louder. "Dorothy's not too good at descriptions, but I kind of figured it was you."

"Keep going south and you'll see a red light. There's a turnoff there, a dirt road. Drive in toward the light. You'll come to a big vacant lot and a bar, but there's no sign. They call it the Shotgun Shack. Meet me there."

"I don't know, Mrs. Belmont."

"What don't you know? I thought you were a smart girl who knew everything."

Barbara leaned in close, her breath against Mary's neck.

Mary stared straight ahead, grinding the steering wheel in her hands. She swallowed hard. "It's late and I really should be getting home."

"Either follow me or I follow you home."

"What was it again? Never mind. I remember, the Shotgun Shack. All right."

Barbara led the way. She turned onto the bumpy road and followed it through scrub desert to a rickety wooden building that looked like a Western saloon. It had a hitching rail outside, a plank sidewalk along the front, and batwing doors.

A sign in the window boasted in blue neon of the breadth of its offerings: *Whiskey, Beer & Nuts.*

Six ghosts sat at the bar. Dungeon dark. On the wall opposite the bar hung a painting of an enormous woman sprawled across every corner of a Victorian couch. She was nude, and by her expression, proud as could be. A bumper sticker on the mirror behind the bar said, *Silence Is Golden, but Duct Tape Is Silver.*

Barbara and Mary sat back near the jukebox and the bathrooms, where the hot air from the open back door rushed in. Barbara had on her black sunglasses and a hoodie that covered most of her face. She looked like a police sketch of the Unabomber.

Mary fidgeted on her barstool, too nervous to talk. Barbara started.

"I want you to know something. That cash you're piping off, I don't care. I don't give a shit you're stealing from Henry."

"You're not—not mad?"

"I should be, don't you think? Mad as hell. You wiggling around in front of my husband and taking his money?"

"I am so sorry. Oh, my God. It's just that Dorothy, her prescriptions, they're so expensive and there are things she needs that I can't afford. Henry doesn't pay me enough to keep up and I—I just..."

"Slow down, sugar."

"I've never done anything like this is my life. I've never stolen anything, ever. I've been exemplary in every way. I feel terrible. It's just that I'm—I'm in an awful bind."

"You don't steal other girls' husbands either, but here we are."

"What?! No! I'd never. Please. I swear to you, Mrs. Belmont."

"Keep your voice down. People know me."

Barbara Belmont did commercials for Belmont Construction's housing developments. On TV, she talked fast, used tons of makeup, and dressed in her best Saturday night clothes. She sat on several charity boards and that raised her profile, too.

The bartender brought drinks, a bourbon neat for Barbara and a Coke for Mary. He had a thin face, a goose neck, and glasses perched atop his hairless head. His sleeves were rolled up. The hair on his arms was black and thick and so finely layered it gave Barbara the creeps.

She pulled out a Marlboro and lit it.

The bartender saw. "No smoking in here, lady. There's a law."

Barbara got a twenty from her purse and flattened it on the bar. When the bartender reached for it, Barbara yanked it away and blew smoke at him. He gave her a dirty look and drifted away.

"Let me ask you, Henry's money, what're we talking, like ten grand? Somewhere around there? How much have you got piled up?"

Mary lowered her eyes and Barbara knew what that meant.

"Twenty?"

Softly, sheepishly: "Keep going."

"No way. How much? Fifty?"

Mary grinned and shook her head.

"You're stepmother must be in tough shape. That's a lot of prescriptions, poor thing."

"You'd be surprised what they cost."

"Bowled over."

"Honestly, Mrs. Belmont, honestly—" Mary paused and breathed in and out, trying to sound strong. "I work hard managing your husband's campaign. I take work home weekends. I work sixty hours a week, sometimes more. Your husband and I have a professional relationship and I do a professional job."

"Easy, sugar. I'm not here to bust you."

"I'm really good at my job."

"You think that impresses me?" Barbara sipped her drink and held up a finger. "The Glock in your desk drawer, now that impresses me. Fully loaded and, judging by the smell, recently fired."

"You went through my things, too?"

"A .45 can screw up somebody's whole day. I happen to know about this stuff."

"I bought it myself. It's totally legal."

"Did you know Henry carries a gun sometimes? When he's out meeting with these fat-cat turds, here and there, different places. The turds don't know he's the turd king. Which I find very amusing. Beretta Nano. Nice little piece."

"I'm a woman alone in the city. I wanted some protection for when I'm carrying Henry's money around."

"You mean your money. I hope you know how to use it."

"There's a pistol range on Bell Road I go to when I'm stressed-out. My dad was a cop. He taught me to shoot." She shrugged. "Shooting relaxes me. It's fun."

"I'm starting to like you. But when it comes to smarts, forget it."

Mary felt the sting of the insult. "Do you know where I took my college degree?"

"Henry promised to dump me so you two can be together. Have I got it right? Should we cue the soft jazz? Some Miles Davis?"

"Really, Mrs. Belmont, I don't know who you think I am."

"The answer to that, it came to me sudden. I was thinking about it and all of a sudden there it was. I realized you're stealing money from a guy you think you have a future with. Sugar, this is unbelievable. We're practically sisters."

"Sisters."

"I know exactly who you are, a tramp just like me. A girl that's full of greed, a girl that likes money and sex and lots of both and has no honest way to get either one. So you get it however. This innocent-fawn routine..."

Barbara's eyes roamed Mary's body. "Personally, I don't get it, but a lot of people seem to think you're a hot property."

"I got where I am because I'm smart. I went to Winchester College." Mary raised her eyebrows. "In Boston?"

"Majored in French art and history. Poetry club, lacrosse. I like lacrosse. Running around in those pretty little outfits bashing people with sticks. Better believe I like lacrosse." Barbara snickered. "Finished second in your class and was probably pissed to hell and back you weren't number one. Got your name on a bunch of honor society lists. Want me to name them?"

"Excuse me, but may I ask how you know all that, Mrs. Belmont?"

"Know where I went? Nowhere. College of nowhere, class of nothing. How do you like that? Won a beauty contest and thought I was somebody. Quit high school, bought a new outfit, and started looking around."

Barbara took a drag on her cigarette. "I admire what you're doing. Making your way in the world. I came up the same way. But tell me, if you're so smart, why do you let Henry walk all over you?"

"He doesn't— No. Don't say that. Sometimes he gets upset but that's just because of the campaign. Henry's under a great deal of pressure."

"He's a jerk." Barbara puffed and sipped her drink. "Wouldn't hurt, you telling him that now and then."

"I can't do that."

"Why not? You're stealing his money. Can't be anything worse than that."

"It's not face-to-face. Looking him in the eye. I just—I don't want to ruin our plans."

Barbara scoffed. "You don't understand men, sugar. Not even a little, and I can help you there. I can give you an advanced course, my asshole SATs."

"It's not like that. When Henry wins, we're going to Washington, DC. We're going to change this country. I'm going to be part of something big."

"Yikes."

A man at the other end of the bar shouted gibberish. The guy next to him shouted gibberish back and shoved the loudmouth off his stool. The fallen soldier stayed sprawled on the floor, laughing, and trying to get up and failing, until the shover and a helper yanked him back onto his stool.

After playfully slugging one another, the three of them went back to their drinks as if nothing had happened.

"Are you going to tell Henry? About the money?"

"Keep the dough, I won't squeal."

"It looks like he's going to win this primary anyway. He won't even miss it. I suppose I should thank you, Mrs. Belmont, but under the circumstances..."

"I got a plan in mind for you. Wanna hear it?"

"A plan."

The bald bartender came. He stood back, didn't spread his hands on the bar, and didn't make eye contact. Barbara ordered fresh drinks. The bartender kept his grinder shut and left.

On the juke, Patsy Cline sang "I Fall to Pieces."

"Use Henry's money for plastic surgery. Get that nose of yours straightened out. That's step one."

"My nose." Embarrassed, Mary covered her nose with her hand. "I guess it is a little— I've never liked it, really. It's the family inheritance."

"Get your boobs done, too. You're lacking the goods upstairs."

"What are you saying? Are you serious?"

"You're like a seventh-grade boy up there." Barbara cupped her hands under her breasts and pushed up. "Double trouble. You'd be surprised. After that, when Henry dumps you, you can walk into any job you want."

"Based on my looks? I won't do it. It doesn't work that way anymore."

"Got news for you, men still run the world, and they like good-looking girls. We have this conversation a hundred years from now, it'll be the same story."

"We've moved past that. That's not the way it should work, anyway."

"Ideals? Is that what we're talking about? Sugar, you're banging Vin the Chin. There are no ideals."

Mary's face paled in embarrassment, and her voice dropped. "Okay, I lied. I did, and I'm sorry. I am so sorry. But it just—I don't know—every day—working together—it just happened."

"So did the *Titanic*."

"Henry is so good-looking and smart."

Barbara flapped her lips. "We talking about the same man?"

Out the back door, visible only by starlight, was a corral holding several long-eared mules. Every few minutes one of them would toss its head and bray.

Barbara rolled her eyes. "I feel sophisticated just being here."

"Not me, Mrs. Belmont. I actually feel a little sick."

"I can see this is going to take some work. I want you to pay close attention. Okay? Listen up. You think you're special, but you're not. Henry's a user, always has been. I'm trying to keep you from putting your money down on the wrong pony, that's all."

"You did, Mrs. Belmont. I'm sorry to say this, but you married him. He's your husband."

"Henry and me, it's over." Barbara puffed, threw her wrist, and blew like a smokestack. "Tall, dark, and stupid quit working for me."

"I'm sorry. I truly wish things were different for you."

"It's been a long time coming. I show up at campaign events to meet the money crowd, make contacts. During the day I'm running the business."

"That sounds like a lot."

"It's a shit ton. Henry's never there so I'm having to learn everything. I'm doing okay, but I mean, it's tough. My cash flow sucks. And when I say 'flow,' think toilet. I'm having to learn zoning, all that stuff. But I like it, you know, it's all my thing."

"That's what I want. I want to make decisions."

"Henry won't allow it. Everything's gotta be about him. My advice, dump him before he dumps you, because it's coming. Soon as he wins, he'll find somebody else."

"He wouldn't do that. Never."

"Step two, hear the rest of my plan."

Mary looked away. "This is—oh—this—oh—I didn't expect all this to happen tonight. I'm trying not to be—all upset."

"I've been exactly where you are, sugar, and have a way out. You need to listen to what I have to say."

"I don't know, Mrs. Belmont. I need time to think."

"Your choice." Barbara squashed out her cigarette and got up to leave. She slapped another twenty down on the bar. "Don't stay here too long. That's one of the lessons in my SATs. Place like this, these rodents won't leave you alone."

CHAPTER EIGHT

Henry's big day had arrived. He'd changed clothes three times, changed bola ties more than that. He had more than a hundred on a rack in his closet and added to his collection all the time. Every few months he'd drive up to Garland's Indian Jewelry in Sedona to check out the new offerings.

When he found a silversmith he liked, he'd visit the Navajo Reservation or the Hopi Reservation and buy directly from the artist. Spreading cash around that way made him popular in Indian Country. Navajos called him the big *bilagáana*.

The slides on his ties were all of different designs and shapes. He had an image of the Navajo Yei, the Holy One. He had the Man in the Maze from the Tohono O'odham, a Hopi snake dancer, and an Apache Gaan dancer.

At Barbara's suggestion, he bypassed all those and chose the Monument Valley design. Above the soaring yellow mesa were turquoise stars and a coral moon. But he needed convincing. Barbara reassured him that he'd made the right choice.

"Everyone recognizes Monument Valley. You can't lose."

"There's no doubt about that, from all those shoot-'em-up movies."

"It's a symbol of the West. You look like an authentic Westerner."

Early morning. Henry and Barbara were in the kitchen of their mansion on Eagle Dancer Drive. It had a butler's pantry, a wood-beam ceiling, and a center island with a black granite countertop as big as an aircraft carrier.

Henry couldn't stop fussing about the tie. He checked it in the glass door of the oven. "One thing's certain, this is the first thing they'll notice. Maybe it'll help break the ice with these people."

A crew from CBS News in Washington had flown out to interview him. Set for 1:00 p.m. at the office. He bent into his reflection again. He jiggled the slide and licked his fingers and matted down his hair.

"Are you sure about this, Barb? I don't think Mary's going to like it. She's got ideas about how to do this and I'm sure a bola tie ain't part of it."

"You have to stand out. Who is this girl telling you how to dress, anyway?"

"I put her in charge of handling the CBS people."

"I'll bet Monica's thrilled."

"She'll get over it. Mary knows what to do. Ever hear the name Luke Walsh?"

"Congressman Luke Walsh? Massachusetts?"

"First year out of college Mary ran his campaign and won. He's a Republican and he won. In Massachusetts. That's the kind of magic I want. She was in DC with him for a year."

Henry performed well at TV interviews when prepared and when the outfit was local. They don't push. They're puppy dogs, just happy you're talking to them.

But Washington reporters don't play the same way. When a national crew travels a long distance, they're under pressure to make news to justify the expense. They get tough, try to roll up some hot sound.

Henry saw the interview as a big opportunity and desperately wanted to do well. "It could put me over the top. But I got up this morning feeling funny."

"You mean walking funny. Last night was to get you to settle down."

"I don't know, this whole thing, it's got me rattled."

"It was the only way I could get any sleep. You'll get my bill."

"Don't screw it up. That's all I keep thinking. Then you start in about the tie."

"Gee, I hope I didn't wreck your confidence, Henry." Barbara had known exactly what she was doing. She knew Mary would never let Henry wear a bola tie. She lit a cigarette in private celebration.

She sat on one side of the granite island and Henry on the other. Both had mugs of coffee. Barbara finished hers and Henry pointed to it.

"More?"

"Sure."

She slid the mug across the flight deck. He grabbed it. "See, I'm trying. I'm working on this relationship, being thoughtful and all that."

"Helluva thing to see."

"Don't look too long. It's like an eclipse. You'll go blind."

"Hey, that's a good one, Henry. Bravo."

When he turned to the coffeepot, Barbara flicked ashes into his mug.

He filled Barbara's cup, turned around, and handed it to her. But he didn't pick up his own mug. Instead, he turned back to look out the kitchen window at the pool, the cabana, the rock waterfall, and the private hiking trail into the mountain, close enough to touch.

"You know what guarantees that I'll have good luck? Seeing a mountain lion up on those slopes. I haven't seen one in two months, but every time I do, I have a great day."

"Your coffee, Henry. It's getting cold."

When he turned around, she pushed his mug toward him. He grabbed it off the counter and drank. Barbara smiled.

Henry drank three more cups and fussed some more about the tie. He grabbed his binoculars off a hook by the door and scanned the mountain slope, but the lions had taken another day off.

He paced until it was time to leave, and when they got to his office on Thomas, the whole staff was there to greet them. As soon as Monica Gomez saw Henry's Monument Valley tie, her eyes bulged in disbelief.

She made a what-the-hell face at Mary. "Are you kidding me right now? Did you agree to this?"

"I had no idea. This wasn't me. I'll handle it."

"You're bossing this operation, Mary, so I suggest you do."

"I said I'd handle it." Mary tugged on the strings of Henry's tie. "This isn't going to work. No way." Henry gave Barbara told-you-so eyes. Barbara threw up her hands and made a face like she was surprised.

Mary took Henry by the arm and pulled him aside. "You need to dress Washington. I've taken care of everything."

In the utility room, Mary had an elegant dark blue suit ready to go, along with a starched white shirt and a red silk tie. She waited outside the door while he dressed. The staff had gathered around. He emerged, gripping the lapels, posing.

Mary motioned as if introducing him. "Ladies and gentlemen, does this man look like a United States senator?"

The staffers definitely agreed. They gave him an eager round of applause and a few words of encouragement. Only Monica didn't take part. She stood with her arms folded.

Mary moved in for some final advice. "Okay, you look like a Washington man, and really, Henry, it's like ..." She acted like she was speechless. "Now you have to remember to talk Washington. Do you have the list of words I gave you?"

"I studied them. You didn't think I would, but I did my homework." He made his voice sound senatorial. "With respect to Social Security..."

"Good, good. I want to add one. 'Feckless.'"

Henry made a confused face.

"I know. It's a weird word but just go with it. I've been meaning to add it to my list."

"It sounds like something you put lotion on."

"Nobody outside DC has ever heard of it. So you can use it for anything you want."

"What does it mean?"

"Aimless, bad." Mary frowned. "Nobody knows. Doesn't matter. But if foreign policy comes up, say it's feckless and change the subject."

Henry got settled into his big chair. On the wall behind the desk hung the Arizona state flag, a red and yellow sunburst above a blue panel. Next to it was a framed print of a miner in a slouch hat with a pickaxe and a shovel, the image from the state of Arizona's Great Seal.

He wanted both in the shot. He wanted voters to see his devotion to the state.

When the crew arrived, he shook hands all around, squeezing too hard and smiling. He sat back down in his chair to let the makeup guy work on him. Barbara and Mary stood behind the camera, the lights, and the umbrellas.

The other staffers were there, too, shoulder to shoulder, excited, whispering.

The day before, Mary had spoken at length with correspondent Isabella Mendez about the topics she wanted to cover, and Mary relayed the information to Henry. Mendez was charming, easygoing, and surprisingly personal.

She sounded more like a campaign consultant than a reporter. "A substantial part of our audience comes from exactly the demographic you need." Mary listened, nodding, not suspecting anything. She assured Henry he had nothing to worry about.

The first questions were about growing up, his dad's sudden death when he was a boy, his mom stepping up and working three jobs to keep everything together. She'd made sure Henry got involved in sports.

He played high school football and earned a scholarship to the University of Texas. He loved to talk football and dived in.

"Yes, ma'am, I had my whole life mapped out: college ball, the pros. I was a linebacker, all-conference, but I got my knee ripped up against Baylor and that was that. The NFL, gone for me. One hit and it was over. Had to get me a regular paycheck job and rethink my whole life."

Mendez cocked her head in phony sympathy, a top five move in the TV interviewer's handbook. "That must've been tough."

Henry made a regretful clicking sound in his mouth. "Lost a dream in a single moment. You remember days like that the rest of your life."

"But you came back, Mr. Belmont. You fought your way back."

This is money, Henry thought. This is exactly what I'd hoped for.

"Sure did, and do you know why? Woke up after surgery with two people standing over my bed, my mom and Sherry Waterman. Sherry stayed with me all through it. Every morning she got me out of bed and off to rehab when I couldn't do it on my own. Never quit on me, by God, not one time. She runs the Boys Home now and I do everything I can to support her."

"Would it be correct to say you two had something special?"

"Never dated anybody else all through UT. Never saw one of us without the other. We talked about it but never got married. Never could get that horse into the barn."

"It sounds like these women made you who you are."

"You're exactly right." Emotion came into Henry's face, and into his tone, too. "There's no doubt I wouldn't be here without the women in my life."

Standing behind the camera and the lights, Mary nodded in approval. Mendez had set up the perfect opening. Henry saw it and charged in. She was proud of him. Mendez let the gauzy memories roll a while longer.

Then she started in with hard questions on issues she'd never mentioned to Mary.

It was an old trick, also in the top five, and Mary had fallen for it.

"Drug overdoses are surging in Arizona. What do you plan to do about it?"

"Drugs... Listen, when I was young... That issue..." Henry paused to gather himself. "What I think about most are the children, the schools. I want to make sure that children from all backgrounds have that opportunity."

"I asked about drug overdoses. What opportunity are you referring to?"

"To be drug-free. To get a good education."

Mendez waited for Henry to finish his point, but he didn't, so she kept on.

"Let's talk about a related issue. Crime. There's a bill pending in the Senate that's getting a lot of publicity. It sets minimum sentencing guidelines for certain offenses and a three-strikes-you're-out provision that some consider quite harsh. Where do you stand on SB3810?"

"Oh yes. SB3810. I've got the text of it, yes. Somewhere. Rest assured, this crime issue is one I'm deeply concerned about."

Mendez looked confused. "Have you read the bill?"

"There are so many issues... Reading them all..." He cleared his throat. "I've been briefed... My staff... And I want voters to know I'm preparing a statement as we speak."

It went on like that. Henry maintained his empty smile through it all.

Then Mendez asked why he wanted to be a senator and the light in Henry's face switched off. She'd jerked his plug out of the wall and he went blank.

It was bad. One by one, his staffers quietly backed out of the room. They knew what was coming and didn't want to be around to see it. He blubbered until the interview ended.

As soon as the office door closed, Henry jumped all over Mary.

"You said this was going to be easy! That was a disaster! Your preparation was a disaster! This was a national audience!"

Henry pressed his face against hers and screamed. She could see his back teeth. He bent toward her, red-faced. She backpedaled. It went on a long time.

"Henry—I didn't know. Henry, she said—Mendez said ..."

"You made me look like a fool in front of the whole country!"

"It wasn't supposed to go that way. Mendez lied to me."

"This is a catastrophe and it's all your doing."

Monica Gomez stood there watching. She'd never look so satisfied.

Barbara muscled between Henry and Mary. "Calm down, Henry. You're the one who froze like a Popsicle. Don't be such a jerk."

He yelled some more. Barbara pushed her face close to his. "Hey, Henry. Pay attention. Look at me. Good, now fuck all the way off."

Barbara was unafraid and calm, and that always threw him. He didn't know what to say. He walked around in angry little circles. She pulled Mary out to the sidewalk. People and cars were coming and going.

Barbara waited until she could speak with nobody close by. "You can't let him talk to you like that. What did I tell you?"

"When he gets that way, I lock up. I can't think, I can't breathe."

"That's not good enough. You can't let that happen. Ever."

"Did you see his eyes? They were coming out of his head." Mary's heart jumped around in her chest. "Oh, my God, I feel like I'm going to throw up." She bent over with her hands on her knees.

Barbara rested her hand on Mary's back. "What're you afraid of? Tell me. What's he going to do to you that's so bad?"

"I could lose my job. What would I do then?"

"He needs you more than you need him. He'd be lost without his female brain. He doesn't know how to do half the stuff you do."

"That's for sure. I keep his schedule. I keep him on time. He'd never be on time for anything if it wasn't for me. I don't just manage the campaign, I do everything for him. I look for cigars, for crying out loud."

"That's right. You're indispensable, so act like it."

Mary blew her nose, a wet, clogged-drain sound.

Barbara waited, letting her clean up before continuing. "Did you see what I did in there? Backing him down? Next time, I want you to do the same. Get right up on him and tell him to fuck off."

"Just like that? To his face?"

"The two most useful words in the language."

"I'd really like to, but I don't know, Mrs. Belmont."

"That's supposed to be your future in there." Barbara pointed toward the office. "Is that what you want? The other thing, you need to hear me out on my plan. The time has come."

"I've been thinking a lot about that."

"Let's get a drink. Shotgun Shack."

"I could use one. But I shouldn't, I really can't. No, no, no, no."

"Twenty minutes."

"Oh, all right."

CHAPTER NINE

They got there just before 3:00 p.m. Coming in the door, they got hard stares from the five men sitting at the bar. Afternoon drinkers have a job to do and don't like being interrupted at work.

Barbara wore the same hoodie and sunglasses. Mary had on a black skirt, modest heels, and a flower-print blouse. She looked fine and ready for the office except for her face, still pale from her encounter with Henry.

They sat on the same stools. The bar's back door was open, as before, and two men were outside tossing bagel bits to some javelina. The powerful odor of them, like decaying flesh, wafted in the door.

The bald bartender remembered Barbara and Mary. Without being told, he brought a bourbon neat and set it down in front of Barbara and a Coke for Mary. She pushed it away, spilling some.

"Make it tequila."

Barbara curled her eyebrows in amusement. "You're totally bullshit at him, aren't you?"

"He's like ... He's so—so—fucking feckless!" Mary dropped her face onto the bar and dissolved in laughter. Barbara did, too.

When the bartender returned with the drinks, he lit Barbara's cigarette and stood there awaiting further orders. Barbara leaned forward. "Hey, 'keep?" She tossed her head. "This is private business. So dust."

He gave a half bow and left.

"See that right there?" Barbara pointed at the fleeing bartender. "That's respect. You gotta fight for it. Same with any man."

"He ran like a rabbit. You scared him to death."

Barbara raised her drink for a toast. Mary took up her tequila. "This is scary for me. I haven't had a drop of alcohol since college. I had some—trouble."

They clinked glasses and Mary threw back the shot. She didn't make a face or a sound or react as if it were anything stronger than water. All she felt was free.

"Standing up for yourself is a muscle that needs working. It's like going to the gym."

"You belong to a gym, Mrs. Belmont?"

"Please. Like I'm going to pay money to sweat next to some gorilla. But you see what I'm saying. Confidence is a muscle you got to work."

"I know you're right. But I fall apart around Mr. Belmont. It's like he's got a hold on me."

"He's only gonna get worse." "I don't know how much more I can take."

"I'm dead serious about plastic surgery. I know a guy can change your life."

"Mrs. Belmont, I shouldn't even be having this conversation." She gave a nervous laugh. "Changing yourself to be attractive to men. No. Absolutely not. It's wrong to objectify. Everybody knows that."

"You must've taken a seminar."

"At Winchester College we lived by certain ideals."

"Dr. Sergio. I'll introduce you. His hands are so soft, and powerful at the same time. They're instruments of self-improvement. He did some work for me a while back. He's across the line in Nogales, Sonora."

Out the door, the javelina snorted in delight at their evening repast, and the men feeding them snorted back.

"I'm not sure I'd go to a plastic surgeon in a border town."

"No, no, it's fine. Doc's amazing. He specializes in customers on the run, cartel trouble. Cash only, no pesos, no forms to fill out, no questions. Very discreet."

"What'd he do for you? You look so lovely."

Barbara gave Mary a long look, and she didn't flinch. She looked back just as hard.

"Let's just say when the bandages came off, I looked completely different. And I needed to look completely different. I was hearing footsteps."

"I don't understand."

Barbara waited. Mary waited. She had an expectant expression that said she wanted Barbara to talk. At first Barbara didn't want to, but she gave in.

"Yeah, all right. I got mixed up with a mobster back east and things didn't turn out. They made me testify and after that I had to scoot. I lammed, like, fast. Packed a bag and adios."

"He was after you?"

"Slept in my car, cheap motels. Paid cash for everything, wore wigs and makeup. I got really good at looking like somebody else. Then got hooked up with a guy called John Sunrise."

"Sounds innocent but I'm guessing he wasn't."

"He disappears people, sets them up with a whole new identity, new name, new backstory, the works."

"Your life should be a movie, Mrs. Belmont."

"John Sunrise sent me to Dr. Sergio. Tells me, 'This is the guy you need to see.' I drove down to Nogales and we did business."

"May I ask who this mobster was?"

"No, you may not. I shouldn't have said that much. Mr. Sunrise and Dr. Sergio got me out of a fix. That's all you need to know."

One of the pros got off his stool and fed some coins into the jukebox. "Satisfaction" by the Rolling Stones came on. On the way back, he gave Barbara and Mary an annoyed stare while singing along in a loud voice. Barbara watched him go. She thought about telling him to scram but didn't want to start something.

"I was lovely back then, too. About your age. Fourteen years ago. But I didn't get the work done to fix nothing. I did it to stay alive."

"I'm trying to picture you at my age."

"You better believe heads turned, and they can for you, too. I mean even more. Part one is Dr. Sergio. Then give Henry the happy digit and walk away. I want you to come work for me."

"Are you serious? Geez, I didn't expect that." Mary wrinkled her face in doubt. "Working for you, I don't know."

"What? Not good enough for you?"

"I appreciate it, really, but I didn't study at one of the elite women's colleges in the country to build houses. No offense, but it's—ordinary. That sounds terrible, but I always thought I'd do something creative."

"You wanna make money, don't you?"

"Why, sure."

"With me working these dumb guys and your smarts, we can turn Belmont Construction into one of the biggest outfits in the West. I'm thirty-nine and ready to make real money, but I need help, somebody to wear the green eyeshades. Me and you working together, we'd make buckets."

"That does sound appealing. But what about Henry?"

"If he fusses, I can sink him overnight. One call to a reporter and Vin the Chin is Vin the loser. He'll keep his yapper shut. Besides, Henry'll be in Washington screwing other girls and you won't be there, so what's the problem?"

"Other girls?" Mary stiffened. "What're you saying?"

Behind them, the mules brayed and the javelina snorted. The smell of them got worse.

"Don't tell me you think you're the only one."

"Well, yes, I did. I thought I was." Mary had a shocked expression. "Who? No, never mind, don't tell me. I don't want to know. Whatever. Are you sure? I don't believe you."

"Sorry to break this to you, but our Henry's a player. He's got a tailor he uses, rigs his britches up with pulleys for easy removal. No shit."

The bartender brought another round. Mary threw back her tequila, and before the bartender could walk away, she wiggled the glass for another.

"I'm feeling all swimmy." She put her hand to her forehead. "What am I even doing?"

"It's okay. If you're around Henry long enough, you'll drink copious amounts. I think that's written down somewhere, like on a canyon wall on the reservation. I should keep up."

Barbara drained her bourbon and handed the glass to the bartender. "Faster this time, 'keep. And set up my friends." She tossed her thumb to indicate the javelina feeders out back. "Whatever they want and as fast as you can pour."

"Hey, you mooks." Barbara spun around on her stool. "Yeah, you. I've had enough of the stench. I set you up for a round. Come in and have a drink on me and shut the door."

They blew inside like tumbleweeds.

Mary was fixated on her troubles. "I got up this morning thinking I could never do anything bad to Henry and he'd never do anything bad to me. That he loves me, and I love him, and everything is good, and he'd never betray me. Isn't that the way it's supposed to be?"

"That's the way love songs go, yeah."

"Now you tell me this, and all of a sudden, I'm having a—bad thought, some déjà vu." Mary's words came out thick. Her head bobbed slightly. "I shouldn't have bad thoughts, but I do. Always have."

"What? Tell me. Bad is sort of my area."

"Can't. No." She shook her head hard to rearrange the furniture in there. "You know how sometimes you crack up a little and have these ideas? They flash through your brain and they're gone just as quick, and you're all right again?"

"Come on, we're just talking here. Two gals chopping it up."

"Revenge. I like getting revenge. It's a thing for me."

"You? Mary Rose Cleary? You're all sorts of interesting, aren't you? All these layers."

"There was a girl at Winchester. She turned on me and I didn't handle it too well."

"You were dating?"

"Pretty heavy. I was drinking back then, and that's like—it changes everything for me."

Barbara raised her arm and snapped her fingers. "Keep those drinks coming. We're on a roll over here." She pulled out a smoke and lit it and puffed and fidgeted with the ashtray. She was grinning.

"I wasn't going to say anything, sugar, but I knew. About you, I mean. At the hat dance, when you were walking through the crowd, I noticed how several of the ladies reacted to you and how you reacted to them. A woman knows about another woman. It's built in, like, in our skin."

A moment passed without talk. Everything had changed between them. They both drank.

"I've been thinking that about you, too, Mrs. Belmont."

"Look at you. Three drinks in and you're taking your shot."

"I'm right. I know I'm right."

"What can I say, I'm a traveler in the world. Whatever happens, happens."

The bartender brought their drinks. Barbara held hers up and nodded and so did Mary. They sipped.

"I get what everybody sees in you now."

"You think I'm attractive, Mrs. Belmont?"

"At first, I was like, what's the big deal with this chick? But yeah, I do." Barbara took a long drag on her cigarette. "The thing I don't get is Henry. What are you doing with him? You had a girlfriend at Winchester, so, you know, whatever. I mean, that's your dance."

Mary lowered her eyes, embarrassed. "This part isn't flattering, admitting this. But power is, ah, what am I saying, powerful. That's real smart, Mary. Deep." She gave a little snort. "Being around power. You know what I mean. What can I say, I like it."

"And Henry was nice to you at first, right?"

"And I wanted an ordinary life, a job, a guy. And I wasn't drinking. I had a bad problem back then and—" She held up her shot glass. "Here I am again."

Barbara reached over and rubbed circles on Mary's back. "So stop. Right now. Get in your car, drive home, and go back to being ordinary."

At Barbara's touch, Mary felt the sudden rush of blood. She gave Barbara a side look, hunger in her eyes. "I don't want to."

"Didn't think so. What can we do about that?"

Mary threw down the remainder of her drink. She let out a breathy moan. "Tequila. It isn't even fair."

"My place is out. Hotels are out, too. I get recognized too easy." Barbara squashed out her cigarette and gathered her things.

"Then follow me home."

"What about Dorothy?"

"Don't worry about Dorothy. I'll—I'll flatten her tires or something."

Mary yelped in laughter and so did Barbara. The men at the bar heckled them as they bumped through the batwing doors together, arm in arm.

CHAPTER TEN

They kissed at Mary's front door and for a long time. They banged against one wall and back against the other. They set off the wind chimes, which played a sweet song all over the neighborhood.

Barbara reached up to kill the sound. "I hate wind chimes."

"I love them."

"You would, such a young girl."

"They make the perfect sound to lose your mind to."

The coyotes heard the wind chimes, too, and started up. Their torture screams echoed over the neighborhood. Dorothy heard the disturbance and called from inside the house.

"It's me, Doe." Mary turned to Barbara and put a shushing finger to her lips. "You know where the bedroom is."

Barbara reached up Mary's shirt from behind and unsnapped her bra. "Make it fast." She brought her hands around to the front and started on her belt buckle.

"What're you even doing?"

"You could make me stop, sugar."

Mary didn't make her stop. They pinballed against the walls again. Dorothy calling to her from right behind the door was the only thing that stopped them. Barbara stepped back out of view. Mary tried to put herself back together. She hurried to open the door before Dorothy did.

"Oh, hello there, Doe. What's— Isn't it— Why are you still up?"

"It's not that late. Is something wrong? You look like a hurricane hit you."

Mary's shirt was hanging loose over her skirt. "Oh." Mary tucked it back in.

"You're all flushed."

"Well, my phone, wouldn't you know it, it fell under the seat and I was on my knees forever trying to get it out. I'm Miss Fumble Fingers tonight."

"How was work? And your special man?"

"He's terrific. He really is just—the most terrific—man." Mary's voice trailed off at the end. She could hear Barbara giggling just beyond the doorway.

"I'm dying to hear what's going on between you two."

Mary picked her purse up off the ground and scooped up the things that had fallen out. She shouldered it. "Let's go inside, Doe. It's hot out here. My, oh, my. And how was your day?"

Dorothy grabbed the wheels and turned her chair and threw her hands to roll herself away. Mary left the door ajar for Barbara and followed Dorothy into the kitchen.

"Never mind about my day. I want to hear all about your budding romance."

Mary talked about work. She didn't mention Henry Belmont. Dorothy pressed for details, but Mary kept it vague. She said she was so, so tired and really needed to catch up on her sleep and suggested they talk another time.

"Okay, but when's my TV coming?"

"Tomorrow. I've been tracking it."

"How wonderful. I'm so excited."

"I should get to bed. Good night, Doe."

"Good night."

Mary went down the hall. Barbara was lying naked on the bed, head leaning on her fist, when Mary came in. She stopped in the doorway, startled. "Whoa."

"Hello, Dr. Sergio. Was I lying? He's the patron saint of getting it on."

"I'll say."

"Come over here, girl."

They got the sheets messy.

At the finish Barbara was out of breath. "You definitely ain't a rookie. I'd say Winchester taught you well."

"It was before Winchester, actually."

"Here's what I figure. You did some funky stuff in high school, nothing too much." They were lying side by side. Barbara had her hand on Mary's stomach. "Like in basements, the car. But your first time was college, am I right? I mean, for real?"

"I tried it the other way. We'd drive into town on Saturday nights, but the Boston University students just talk you to death. Tufts, Northeastern, it's all the same. Nothing lonelier than being around college guys. Not one of them could change a tire."

"There's no men anymore."

"I thought it was just me. For the longest long time, seriously." Mary swiped her arm across her forehead to catch the sweat. "Thing is, I liked men and wanted one that knew himself and wasn't always performing. I thought I wanted one, but I really didn't."

"Grabby bozos and little boys, take your pick."

"A lot of us Winchester girls were like that. Starved and willing to try anything."

"I found one that's working out okay." Barbara raised her head. "Wait, you don't mind I got a boyfriend, do you?"

"No, not really. It surprises me, though. A little, I guess. Yeah."

"He's a cop. Young, on the rise, smart."

"Good-looking?"

"Oh, darling, let me tell you, he's gorg. The sex is ridiculous, and he treats me good."

"Now, that surprises me."

"Work. I'm talking about work. Tony helps out with contractors, suppliers. If they need a visit or a talking-to, he takes care of it. He listens to me and people listen to him."

"That's wonderful, Mrs. Belmont."

"Says he loves me, too. Where'd that come from, right?"

"You love him?"

"Let's not go nuts."

"That makes me feel better."

"It's just business, sugar, and business is good." Barbara sat up and put her hand to her forehead. She was dizzy. "Whoa. After that, walking is going to be a major challenge. If I can manage it, I might try making it to the little girls' room."

She looked at the row of faces under the cowboy hats on the shelf. "I don't know how you sleep with those things staring at you. You put all those faces on?"

"I like to draw. I don't know, they're my friends, if that doesn't sound too weird."

"It's deeply weird, so, yeah." Slowly, on wobbly legs, Barbara got out of bed and went over to the hats and put one of them on. It was black and flat-brimmed with a rounded crown. She pointed to the face, which had a stubble beard and huge whiskey eyes. "Who's the dude?"

"Buckskin Frank Leslie. He was an army scout and saloon man in Tombstone."

"I'd wear the Buckskin Frank." Barbara put her hands on her hips and posed. She was naked and enjoying it. She still looked good, even with the start of a small roll around the stomach. Her shoulders had a nice round shape, her hips flared perfectly, and she was bouncy up top. "These are all from Henry's rallies?"

"I'm running out of room. But I like having them."

"With those things staring at me, I wouldn't sleep five minutes. They're like a jury of my peers and I don't have any peers. So what chance would I stand?"

Barbara put the Buckskin Frank back on its head and started into the bathroom. On the way she pointed to the bureau. "Your hidden safe? You call that hidden? Ain't so hidden, is it?"

"Is it that obvious?"

"Those drag marks on the rug are like a map. Anybody that comes in's gonna see them."

"Sometimes I forget to brush them out."

Barbara went into the bathroom, shut the door, and sat on the toilet. In a loud voice: "You never did tell me how much you have in that safe. I'm curious."

"I never really counted."

"Don't give me that. Girl, with your brains, you know exactly how much."

"I don't want Doe rolling up on me. I think she's trying to figure out my combination. She's always asking questions about Mr. Belmont. When I come in here with cash, I toss it in fast as I can."

"Just shut the bedroom door."

"I've caught her listening outside. Better to keep it open so I can hear her coming."

"I know it's more than fifty grand."

"You underestimate me, Mrs. Belmont. When I put my mind to something."

"Listen to you, a proud thief. Go ahead and open it up."

"I don't know."

The toilet flushed. Barbara used the sound as cover to open the medicine cabinet, an old habit. Checking people's prescriptions gave her an edge. It held all the usual items, no drugs of note.

Whose medicine cabinet doesn't stash mind-altering substances? That's concerning.

Just as quietly, she looked inside the vanity underneath and found nothing of interest there either, only cleaning materials.

There's something seriously wrong with this girl.

She turned on the water in the sink and raised her voice over it. "I'm fine with you having a nest egg. Far as I'm concerned you earned it, shoveling Henry's horseshit every day. It's all yours."

Barbara turned off the water, dried her hands, and walked out of the bathroom. "Come on, what's the combination?"

"Nobody's supposed to know."

"It's me." Barbara Belmont spread her hands. "I'm naked in your bedroom. You need ID?"

"You'll laugh at me. You already think I'm a fool about Henry."

"Why would I laugh? Come on, I promise I won't laugh."

"The combination, really, I'm so embarrassed. It's his birthday."

Barbara shouted out a belly laugh.

"See, what did I tell you? You promised."

"I've been there, believe me." Barbara laughed so much she had to dry her eyes with her fingertips. "What a world. Sometimes you can't make it up."

"What? It's not that funny."

"Nothing."

"It's something."

"I said it was nothing." Barbara gave a sharp look and held it. Those slicing eyes gave Mary a chill. Barbara went to the open bedroom door and peered down the hall. "No Dorothy. Let's go, open it up."

Mary couldn't say no. She dragged the bureau across the carpet, removed the panel in the wall, and got down on her heels. She punched in the numbers, opened the safe, and scooped up the cash in fistfuls.

They counted it on the bed, and the higher the amount went, the more excited Barbara became. Her hands began to tremble when the number topped $105,000.

"Why, you lousy crook. I underestimated you." Barbara smiled, happy again.

"I didn't realize it was that much."

"Quite a gig you got going. Must be nice having a boss trust you as much as Henry." Barbara closed the bedroom door and threw the bills in the air and let them flutter to the mattress until they covered it corner to corner. She was giddy. "Let's roll around in it. Feel what it's like to lie in a bed of stolen money."

"I'm not doing that, Mrs. Belmont. Money's gross, it's filthy."

"So are we. Don't think you're any better, Miss Winchester. You're a grifter. You pretend you're not but you got real talent. You find the soft spots. You knew how much was in that safe all along, didn't you?"

"Told you. I never counted it because of Dorothy."

"You're a lousy liar. You gotta work on that." Barbara pushed a strand of hair out of Mary's eyes. "But you know what? I forgive you."

Barbara started up again, and so did the wind chimes. She rolled on top.

"Don't. I'm all sweaty." Mary sucked in a breath. "Oh, oh, yes. Right there." She moaned. "All this beautiful money."

"Sticks like cheap wallpaper, don't it?'

CHAPTER ELEVEN

Nobody could miss Dusty Rusty's Hat Emporium on Scottsdale Boulevard. On the sidewalk outside stood a ceramic statue of a cowboy twirling a rope. Buckaroo Bill stood twelve feet tall and had a goofy smile. His clothes were painted bright red and blue. He wore a yellow scarf and his Wranglers were tucked into his boots.

The owner put a different cowboy hat on Bill's head every morning, his daily special. Today it was a classic cattleman's model, white and high-crowned with a trough in the middle.

Master hatmaker Freddy Ayala met Mary Cleary at the front door. He took her into his workshop in back to show off his latest work, a black gambler with a low, circular crown, a flat brim, and a horsehair band.

He turned it in his hand. "If you give me another day to shape it, I'll have this beauty ready to go out the door. It'll grab some eyes."

"That sounds exciting, Freddy, but I'm in a hurry. I need one right now."

"I'll have the gambler ready for next time. You tell folks that's genuine horsehair, and I guarantee they'll pony up."

"We need it. The big day is getting closer."

"Let's see what's on the rack."

They went out to the sales floor. Rows of hats hung on spikes on the walls. The spaces between them were decorated with ropes, spurs, brands, and bridles, as well as black-and-white photos of rodeo cowboys in every stage of flailing flight from the backs of bucking bulls.

Wearing a brown leather apron with tools in the front pockets, Freddy stayed at her shoulder as she tried on hats. He had a nice smile and a modest mustache. He was tall and heavyset, his girth packed in under the apron.

Mary tried on a black wool hat with a three-crease crown. Freddy reached up and used the tips of his fingers to tilt the hat to one side for a perfect sit.

"I'm proud of this one. That headband I made out of repurposed reins. Rodeo cowboys want the curled brim so it doesn't get in the way when they're roping, see." He twirled his arms overhead to demonstrate.

"I won't be roping anything but dollar bills. For the hat dance, I'll need a deeper crown."

"It'll be like a challenge to fill it up. I get it. That's smart. It sounds like Mr. Belmont is on his way."

"You bet. We both are. Together."

She mugged in front of the mirror in different models before selecting a buck-colored felt Stetson with diamond-shaped coral stones on the band.

"You can't go wrong with that one, Miss Cleary. European rabbit fur, a smooth finish, and the felt is good and tight."

"I think I love it."

"We call that the Ox Bow. You'll look dandy in that one."

"You think so?" Mary ran her fingers back and forth along the brim, turning her head this way and that. "You know what, Freddy? I love it."

"Ain't cheap, three fifty plus the governor's cut."

"Seems like the fancier the hat, the more we collect."

"That's because it sends a message. Quality does."

"I don't think Mr. Belmont would mind. I'm feeling good today, Freddy. Better than I have in a long time. This is the one for sure."

"Terrific. I'll box her up."

Mary left. As she drove to the site of the speech, Henry Belmont called telling her to go to a lawyer's office to pick up a pouch of money. "Usual arrangement. Someone will approach the car."

"Hello to you, too, Henry."

"Where are you?"

"I bought a really expensive hat, just to let you know. But I look exquisite in it and I think the crowd will love it." She didn't say the price. She waited for him to ask, but he didn't.

"As long as you fill it up. What about my Cohibas?"

"Henry, I haven't even had breakfast."

"Get going on it. It's important." He was always scattered and grouchy in the morning. "All right, now, about this pouch."

"How much?"

"Fifteen. My 'throw' phone beeped with pickup instructions. I just texted them to you. Take care of it with the fat man and get to the theater as early as you can."

Henry had a rally at the Territorial Theatre downtown. The pickup spot was a law firm on Camelback Road south of the Biltmore Sanctuary. The massive pink building had stone gargoyle faces etched into its facade and domes on the multilevel roof.

Mary's instructions were to wait in the parking lot, and someone would approach the car. She called Frankie Santiago to alert him of a coming deposit and sat there, tapping the steering wheel and looking around.

Thinking the messenger might've been looking for a different car, she got out and stood against the Corolla. The heat beat down on her. She stuck to the car as the time stretched to more than an hour.

Stand out in the heat long enough and you see the faces of dead relatives, and they're all having more fun than you.

Her phone beeped with a text from a blocked number. The instructions had changed: "Walmart, Village Crossroads on Cactus Road. North lot. Right now and stay in the car!"

Mary got into the Corolla, blasted the air-conditioning, and stuck her face against the vents. When she could think straight again, she drove to the Walmart and parked and stayed put in the car. She watched people coming and going.

She watched a blue-vested geezer wrestle an unruly conga line of carts.

Someone knuckled on the passenger window. When she rolled it down, a huge man with a bushy beard, flabby arms, and coveralls dropped a pouch onto the seat.

He leaned down with his head sideways, never looking in at her. "You're supposed to stay in the car. Eyes everywhere. Next time follow orders."

Mary counted the money. She peeled off $4,000, put it into an envelope, and put the envelope in her purse. She put the remaining $11,000 into a separate envelope.

I can't believe you're not more careful, Henry. Serves you right.

CHAPTER TWELVE

Mary drove to El Toreador. Fat Frankie stood outside dressed nicer than usual in pressed beige slacks and loafers without socks. His button shirt was a pink Patagonia with black alligators on it. On the way to the bank he pressed Mary on when they'd get together.

"You don't give up, do you?"

"I can't get you off my mind. I'm a wreck."

"You look like you're doing fine, Frankie."

"I'm dying over here. I'm scared I'll have a heart attack."

"Now you're being dramatic, like you're up onstage. Frankie the thespian."

"I'm on the verge. Say you'll think about it. That'll be enough to hold me over so I don't expire on the spot."

"Oh, stop it. I told you before I'd think about it."

Mary felt in control with Frankie and liked it, especially after Henry. She had no fear and every word came out right, just the way it sounded in her head.

After dropping Frankie at the restaurant, she drove home and stashed the $4,000 in her safe and drove downtown to the theater on Adams Street. She found a parking spot three blocks away and hurried down the sidewalk wearing the Stetson.

The Territorial Theatre was a refurbished early-twentieth-century opera house. The marquee sticking out over the box office had Henry Belmont's name on it. She was a half hour late. People milled around outside and she could hear the crowd clapping rhythmically inside, eager to get the speech underway.

If Mary didn't show up with the hat, Henry's signature grand finale wouldn't happen, and he couldn't begin until she got there. The way they choreographed the show, her appearance had to be a surprise. The crowd couldn't see her until Henry had made his big introduction and she came striding down the middle aisle.

That meant she couldn't go in the front door.

She went around to the alley in back and pounded on the door and kept pounding until a stagehand opened it. Barbara was waiting right there and Henry, too, and he was angry.

"I never keep my audience waiting! Never!"

"The delivery got messed up. I had to go to two places."

"Do you know how many people are out there waiting on me? There's three hundred people out there. They're bankers, finance people. They vote! They have money!"

"There was so much traffic. I caught every light."

"They're about to leave. They're about to walk out. I can't lose these people. Five more minutes and they would've walked out."

The more Henry talked, the madder he got. He waved his arms and tried not to not shout. Mary tried to explain, but the words tangled up on her lips.

The emcee began the introduction. The red velvet curtains opened and it was like somebody had flipped a switch. Henry mopped his face with a handkerchief, pasted on a smile, and walked out to loud applause.

Barbara watched him begin and turned to Mary. "You didn't do it. You didn't tell him to fuck off."

"I'm doing the best I can, okay?"

"You gonna be able to do your act? You can't go out there upset and blubbering all over the place. And you're sweating."

"That's because I was in a hot car. And I don't blubber. I'm fine." Mary spat out the words. "I don't know why I get so weak around him. It makes me sick. Don't ever say I blubber, Mrs. Belmont."

"There you go. Try working some of that attitude on Henry."

"Sorry, I don't mean to take it out on you."

"It's good practice. Never apologize to a man. That's on page one of my lesson plan."

"I'm supposed to get him cigars. Cohibas. What do I know about Cuban cigars? It's never enough with him."

"I'll handle the cigars. You look like you're about to lose your cookies."

"I'm not myself today. My head is absolutely screaming." Mary's jaw hung open and she was out of breath. "What even happened last night? Don't tell me, I don't want to know. God."

"You had some lady fun."

"I was so drunk. That shouldn't have happened."

"Go easy on yourself. A girl needs to get blotto now and then." Barbara had her lipstick tube out and was primping at her reflection in the small window of a stage door. "If I drink too much wine, next morning in the mirror I go, 'Who's that scary broad?' Takes an hour to get the roadkill out of my eyes."

She glanced over her shoulder. "You didn't forget what we did last night, did you?"

"I didn't forget."

"Nobody does with me. I know how to cha-cha-cha." She pumped her arms. "We on for another round tonight?"

"I don't know what to say right now except I'm sorry. It shouldn't have happened. Last night was a mistake. I wouldn't be where I am if it wasn't for Mr. Belmont."

Henry's amplified voice echoed around the auditorium.

"Yeah? Where's that, exactly?"

Mary shook her head, upset, confused, lost. "I don't even know."

"You'll be back."

Henry gave his regular speech. Mary pulled herself together and performed the hat dance well. When the show ended, Barbara went to the lobby to work the crowd as they exited. She shook hands and said hello to old friends and tried to make new ones.

Mary and Henry went back to the office. He raged around like a madman. Mary wanted to explain but couldn't get any words out. She tried to distract him by showing him the money they'd collected.

The haul totaled $2,200. He grabbed the stack and fingered it, and it calmed him. He peeled off five twenties for himself and handed the remainder back to Mary.

"Split it the usual way, between the library men and the Boys Home."

"It's too late to get to the bank and Sherry Waterman's probably gone for the day. It'll have to be first thing in the morning."

"Yeah, yeah, fine."

Upset at the way things had gone, Mary wanted to stay to talk to Henry and put things right. She knew she wouldn't sleep if she didn't. She tried, but Henry said he had more work to do and told her to go home.

CHAPTER THIRTEEN

Driving along, with Barbara's words echoing in her ears, Mary became angry at herself, upset at her cowardice. She remembered how Barbara had handled the bartender, and how much she admired her for it. She wished she could do the same with Henry.

She worked out what she wanted to say and practiced it out loud until she was confident that she could speak without tripping on her words. Almost home, she swung into a U-turn and drove back to the office.

Another car was parked in Mary's usual space.

Approaching the front door, she heard a disturbance at the office window. She walked toward the sound, heard the blinds rattling against the glass, and stepped closer to peer in through the side crack.

What she saw gave her a jolt. Her stomach turned over. Unsure what to do, she hurried back to her car and sat behind the wheel. She was shaking all over.

You were right, Mrs. Belmont. I had no idea. How could I not have known? How could I have been so foolish?

She started the engine, peeled out of the lot, and knifed into the traffic on Thomas, forcing cars to swerve into the next lane. She gassed it. Two blocks away, her mind in an uproar, she flattened the brakes.

"Not this time, Henry!"

She spun into a U-turn and sped back to the lot. She jumped out of the car, leaving the door open and the engine running, and marched up to the window and pounded on the glass.

"Henry! Henry!" She pounded again, much harder. "Henry, come out here! Henry!" She shouted his name over and over.

He cracked the blinds and stuck an eyeball in the space, and a moment later rushed out the door with his shirt tail hanging out.

"What do you think you're doing?"

"I've got something to say, Henry."

"I can't have you screaming on the sidewalk. That's totally unacceptable behavior. You need to remember something, you work for me." He jammed his thumb into his chest.

"Are you listening?"

"Listening? Listening—to what?"

She put her nose close to his. "Fuck you, Henry!"

He froze and blinked several times as if staring at the noon sun. "Look, Mary, if you'll let me explain. I'm sure we can work this out. First of all, I thought I sent you home. Didn't I send you home? Why are you even here?"

Monica Gomez stepped out the door. Her clothes were rumpled and her makeup smeared. She carried her shoes by her fingertips. "See you tomorrow, Henry." As she tiptoed past, she gave Mary a what-can-you-do? shrug. "Bad timing. So sorry."

Mary's temper burst and she lunged at Gomez, who hurried away chuckling. Henry held Mary back. As this was happening, Barbara pulled into the lot. Mary kept fighting Henry's grip, thrusting her arms over his shoulders trying to reach the shoeless Gomez.

Barbara walked up looking unusually happy. "I was going to watch Turner Classic Movies tonight." She rocked her head and pursed her lips. "But this works."

When Gomez drove away, Henry released Mary. She promptly slugged him in the face. He tried to duck but wasn't fast enough. She landed a good second blow, a solid right that dizzied him. Every swing after that went wild as he ducked and backpedaled, shielding himself with his arms.

"I can't have this! I can't have a lunatic woman fighting me in a public place! What's wrong with you! If this lands on YouTube, I'm finished! Mary, Mary, what's wrong with you!"

Watching, Barbara chuckled, hands on hips.

"Please! Barbara, I'll lose everything! Can't you do something!?"

"About you, Henry, afraid not. About her, sure. I'm getting used to it."

Taking Mary by the shoulder, Barbara pulled her far enough away to let Henry escape into the building.

Barbara couldn't get the smile off her face. "You're moving up in your SATs, sugar. You're in the advanced class now."

Mary's fury put her beyond talking and beyond listening. She stomped off to her car and drove away. Barbara went into Henry's office and marched up and down in front of his desk, calling him names and taunting him as best she could.

She wanted him to feel misery but couldn't break through. She didn't bother with guilt and regret. He was beyond those. By the time she gave up and left, Henry was sipping Horse Soldier with his shoes off and his feet up.

Barbara got in her car and drove to Mary's house.

CHAPTER FOURTEEN

Several cars were parked outside. Big old boats stuck against the curb at crazy angles. No one responded to Barbara's knocks, but she heard voices inside. She opened the door, knocking again as she did, and poked her head inside.

Dorothy and three other women were chattering and sipping cocktails as they sat around the dining room table playing bridge. More voices came from the kitchen, all women. The house smelled like onion dip and old lady.

Barbara walked far enough inside to be seen. She coughed. "Hell-ooo."

Looking up, Dorothy spotted her from across the room and ignored her for a full thirty seconds. "Mary ain't here. Was a minute ago, took off."

"Do you know where?"

"We're in the middle of our auction. It's very serious." Dorothy had a cigarette burning in the corner of her mouth. The other women were too engrossed in their game to even glance at Barbara. "Ladies, it's bidding time, so let's get on with it."

The card players all spoke at once. A woman with a mound of silver hairdresser hair walked out of the kitchen. Holding a drink to her lips, she passed Barbara. "I make a glorious Manhattan. Help yourself, sweetie."

"I'm looking for Mary."

"But why? Everyone's here and the party's on. Welcome to the Salvation Army's granny muster. We never lost a battle, isn't that right, girls?"

In unison, the women in the kitchen and the ones at the table chanted a rhyming ditty. They were all deep-voiced and giggly, and by the end they were laughing uproariously.

"I hate to interrupt, but I really need to find Mary."

"She was here." Manhattan raised her drink in the air. "Offered her one of my famous cocktails and she looked right through me. I'm not saying she was impolite or nothing, but..."

"Yeah, she was." Dorothy's eyes stayed glued to her cards. "She come in like a tornado and went out the same way. Never said, 'Hey there, Dorothy.' 'How are you, Dorothy?' 'So nice to see you, Dorothy.' Never said a word to my friends either. Rude, rude."

"Sorry about that, but can you tell me where she went?"

"Somewhere fast and I dunno. Jimmy crack corn." Dorothy rumpled her lips and laughed from the corner of her mouth that didn't hold a cigarette. "The competition is fierce over here, so if you don't mind."

Barbara had an idea. She remembered Mary saying she went to the shooting range for stress relief. "Thanks anyways. I'll let myself out."

"Before you go, sweetie." With her nose in her glass, Manhattan leaned close to Barbara. "Your nails could use some help." She held up her hand to show off hers. Whispering, confidential: "Between you and me, press-ons. Target." She pronounced it *Tar-jey*.

When Manhattan left to join the group at the table, Barbara walked down the hall to Mary's bedroom. She keyed open the lower right-hand drawer. The Glock was missing.

As she walked out of the house, Barbara used her phone to find the address of the indoor shooting business on Bell Road, and twenty minutes later she pulled up to the Holy Hell Gun Range.

It was 8:00 p.m. and extra dark. Most of the parking lot lights had blown out. The two that worked blinked on and off like an SOS signal. The business was set in a strip mall with a vintage clothing store on one side and a Middle Eastern restaurant on the other.

A sign in the range window said: *Lock your vehicles! Not responsible for items stolen from cars! Be smart!*

Barbara put on her black sunglasses and hoodie and went inside. The front room had rifles hanging on the wall behind the register. There was a glass case stocked with handguns for sale, along with paraphernalia like cleaning kits and concealed-carry holsters.

The counter clerk had an acne-scarred face. He wore an Arizona Diamondbacks ball cap backward, a holstered sidearm, and a tie-dyed T-shirt bearing the image of James Madison.

"Welcome to Hell, miss."

Barbara pointed at the glass partition leading to the shooting room. She walked through the door. All eight lanes were empty except the one Mary was using. Shell casings littered the floor and the room reeked of gunpowder, the rank smell of trouble nobody comes back from.

Barbara stepped into the lane beside Mary. "You never should've looked in that window. Henry's horror show, I call it."

Mary wore earmuffs and her face was pinched in anger. As fast as her trigger finger could move, she squeezed off five rounds at a paper target, the figure of a man.

"Guess you believe me now. Henry has girls all over."

Mary aimed and fired twice more. If she knew she had company, she gave no sign of it. In her total concentration on the target, in the blood intensity of Mary's stare, Barbara saw everything she needed to see.

"You're going to kill him, aren't you?"

Mary fired seven more rapid-fire rounds. She pressed the release button and caught the empty magazine as it fell out. She put the Glock on the counter. She pulled a bottle of tequila from her pocket, twisted off the cap, sipped, and began thumbing rounds into the magazine.

James Madison ran out from behind the glass into the shooting area.

"Excuse me. Miss—miss—we don't allow drinking in here. Did you read the sign? You'll have to put that away."

Mary whipped around and threw him a vicious look that sent knives whistling across the room. Without a word, Madison turned and fled.

"You have to earn respect, isn't that right, Mrs. Belmont?"

"Tequila washes the private school right out of you. I like that."

Barbara put her purse down, fished out a short-barreled revolver, bright silver with a black hand-checkered wood grip, and fired three rounds.

Mary glanced over. "Colt King Cobra .357."

"You know your firearms."

"I do."

"Fits nice into a lady's hand." Barbara squeezed off another shot. "Best of all, it's an orphan, untraceable." She fired twice more. Each bullet broke the heart of the paper man.

Mary was impressed. "You're very good."

"If you're gonna have help, it should be the best."

CHAPTER FIFTEEN

They walked outside. In Phoenix in August, the daytime heat sticks around to prowl the night, burning. Waves of it rushed off the pavement at them.

Barbara glanced at the hazy sky and groaned. "It's hard to breathe. The air is like syrup."

"So put it on your pancakes. Why does everybody talk about it all the time?"

"I can't help it. The heat's on my mind. No matter how low I keep the AC, it's always there, even indoors. Don't you feel that way?"

"I have an evaporative cooler, Mrs. Belmont."

"Ouch. That's hardcore."

"It's Mississippi all summer at my house."

"Guess it makes you cranky? Boy, you're in a mood."

"Are we going to kill Henry Belmont or just talk about it?"

"If it was January, you'd be back wanting to marry him. They'd be fitting you for a white gown right now."

"Are you trying to talk me out of this?"

"You think I don't want Henry dead? The man collects bola ties. He has it coming. But you need to take it easy, sugar."

The heat surrounded them, crowding in, pressing on their nerves. Mary kicked violently at a piece of trash bouncing along on the breeze. She missed and almost lost her balance. Out of breath and needing a distraction, she turned to stare at the traffic humming along on Bell Road.

Barbara gave Mary a minute to pull herself together. "When you're ready, my SUV. We'll go over the details."

"Make it my car. I left the twenty-two hundred in there from the hat dance."

"In your Corolla? In this neighborhood?"

"Can't remember if I locked it either."

"Why didn't you stick it in the safe when you went home to get your gun?"

"I was in a rage. Guess I wasn't thinking."

"This is what worries me. Making lousy decisions when your temper blows. You got yourself a temper, girl."

"What of it?"

"Don't get me wrong, I enjoyed seeing you slug Henry." Barbara chuckled. "But you gotta keep yourself together if we're going to pull this off. If you lose your porridge, we're both going down."

They got into the front seat of the Corolla, leaving the dark city to its infernal plots. Mary swigged from her tequila bottle and offered it to Barbara.

"How are we going to do it?"

Barbara waved off the drink. "I learned a few things in my previous life."

"You haven't told me a thing about that."

"What I know is, it has to be fast and clean. Nighttime, no witnesses, and alibis all set. The first place they look is people close to the, ah, deceased."

"That would be Henry. I want him gone. Cold dead."

Barbara pointed to the tequila bottle. "Maybe you should cut out that neck oil for a few days, make sure your head's right."

"Why do I keep getting the feeling you're backing out on me, Mrs. Belmont? If you haven't got what it takes, leave it to me."

"You can't act reckless on a murder. Get that through your head."

"All I want to know is how we're going to do it."

"If you let me think, I'll tell you."

Barbara took her time. She wore a brassy perfume that didn't mix well with the oily smell of the old Corolla. Cars rolled past on the road behind them, lights streaking and that roaring engine sound coming and going.

"Okay, I got it. Yeah, this sets up nice, the way things work between you and Henry moneywise. He'll move fast if there's a big donation on the line, right?"

"Like a cheetah."

"You do all the money stuff for him, make the pickups, go to the bank, all that. Well, this time the money man wants Henry there when the cash is delivered."

"He won't like that. He keeps a wall up between himself and the money."

"If it's a truckload, he'll go."

"I'll have to tell him who it's from. He'll ask, and I'll need a story. He'll want to know why they won't just give the money to me."

A dark-haired man exited the Middle Eastern restaurant. He closed the door, pulled keys from his pocket, and locked it. He saw the two women in the car behind him, started walking by, turned for a second look, and continued to his car.

Barbara and Mary kept their eyes on him until he drove off the lot.

"Is there somebody Henry's working on, trying to get an endorsement?"

Mary sipped her drink and pondered. She sat scrunched against the door, her knee across the seat and her left hand draped over the steering wheel holding the tequila bottle. She sipped and made a smacking noise and wiped her lips with the back of her hand.

"Yes. Yes, the teachers' union. Sure, those guys have been after him a long time."

"There you have it, very nice. That's what you tell him. This guy from the union wants a face-to-face to explain his concerns.

Happens all the time. Everybody wants to think they're inside, that they got his ear."

"I need to know something, Mrs. Belmont. Who's going to pull the trigger? Because I can do it."

"No, no, no. We have to be smart."

"I swear I can."

"How do you know that? You don't know that, so don't be talking that way. Don't talk like you know about killing when you don't."

Mary started to speak, but Barbara interrupted.

"You won't know until the gun's in your hand whether you can do this or not. That's when the tension surges through your whole body so bad every nerve is screaming. You can't feel your legs and your hands are cold and you don't know if you can even squeeze the trigger. That's when you find out if you have the right blood to kill a man."

"You sound like you've done this before."

Barbara snapped her head toward Mary and gave her a grave look. It had nothing to do with the right or wrong blood. It meant, "Don't ask about my past again."

"Do I at least get to watch?"

"You'll be there, sugar. I'll need you. Most important thing is where. We need a place to do it. Not the office, not home."

"What about a parking lot? He steps out of his car and *bang*. Maybe we can pay a shooter. You must know somebody."

"I'm not bringing anybody in. No matter how good he is, that's one more person can land us at Florence. A parking lot's out, too. It's empty one minute and a second later there's people walking by. Like that guy just now from the abba-dabba joint."

Barbara patted her purse. "No, the only thing I'm bringing is the orphan."

"Okay, so where do we do it, Mrs. Belmont? Where?"

"Gimme a minute to think. You need to stay calm."

"I am calm, I am calm." Mary sipped tequila. "Fuck me, I'm so calm I can't stand it."

The quiet of the car was broken by the scream of a police siren. Mary and Barbara both turned to look.

"Shit."

"Shit."

The black-and-white whipped past, roof lights flashing.

"We need to hurry up, Mrs. Belmont. I don't like just sitting here. Where?"

"There's a lot of ratty motels along the 10. One of them should do it. Can you get him inside a room?"

"If the money's right, I can make him jump out of a plane without a parachute."

"You tell him so-and-so from the union wants a private meeting and it has to be super private. It's a lot of money and he wants a face-to-face first before he hands it over."

"Hold on, who rents the room? Even these rundown motels have video surveillance now. No way I can be seen renting the room."

"One of us has to do it. We need a key to get into a room."

"It's out of the question. I can't."

"A minute ago you offered to shoot him."

"I'm Henry's campaign manager. People know me."

"Any way we do this is risky. How do we get into a room without going to the office and getting a key? We have to be daring."

"I'm daring. But going into the office? Let's ditch the motel room."

"No, a motel works perfectly." Barbara thought the matter over. She bounced her knee and bit her lip in calculation. "Okay, screw it, you don't have to go in the office. I'll do it."

"But it's worse for you. You're so well-known from your TV spots."

"First off, it's no better than fifty-fifty the cameras work. People that stay at these motels don't want cameras. The managers put them up for insurance. And even if they work, I got tons of makeup and wigs left over from when I was on the run. I can make myself look like Marilyn Monroe or a guy that lives in a cardboard box on the sidewalk or anybody in between."

"It sounds like you didn't need Dr. Sergio at all."

"I got tired of putting that paint on and taking it off. Every day for the rest of my life? Dr. Sergio solved that problem."

"Makeup. I suppose that could work."

"You bet it'll work. Here's how it's gonna go."

Mary leaned close. The tequila had flooded into her green eyes. It made them shine in the darkened cab.

"I'll scout around and find a motel. The tricky part is we need two cars, you in one and Henry in his. Can you get him to drive his own car?"

"He won't like that, Mrs. Belmont. Like I said, when it comes to money, he wants to stay hidden."

"He has to be in his own car. The cops find him dead and no car, they'll wanna know how he got there. Somebody had to drive him, so who was it drove? We need to answer that question for them. The more answers we give them, the less they poke around."

"I can do it. Leave it to me. I've got an idea."

"All right, so you two drive into the motel and park far away from the office. Henry won't want to be near the office, in case he's seen, and he'll want you to rent the room, right?"

"Definitely."

"Okay, so he waits in his car while you pretend to go to the office. Only I'll be waiting near there, and I'll go in and rent the room and hand the key to you. But it won't be me, it'll be Marilyn Monroe."

"You mean you'll be dressed up like Marilyn? Like a Marilyn prostitute?"

"Nobody knows it, but years ago, dear old Henry got arrested in a hotel with two bimbos in fishnets. One of 'em was a dolled-up blonde."

"I had no idea. Henry?" She made a disgusted sound. "Boy, he had me so fooled."

"What I know about Henry, I could bury him. That's how come he keeps me around. When he's gone, the cops will dig around, find out about the fishnet twins, and figure he was up to his old crap again."

Mary sipped her tequila. Barbara got a cigarette going, cracked her window a few inches, and blew smoke out. "Ever see those old photos of Marilyn Monroe?"

"I don't know. That was before my time. Maybe one or two."

"Like at the premier of a movie, say, *How to Marry a Millionaire*. I like old movies. Look it up. She's in your Google. She's all decked out and wearing white gloves. That'll be me. White gloves means no prints. No way of proving I was ever there."

"The clerk probably sees weirder stuff every day."

"So I come out of the office and hand you the key and you go back and take Henry up to the room. Get settled and wait for my knock."

"*Tap, tap, tap.* 'Oh, Henry?'"

"'Open up and meet the reaper, lover boy.'"

Mary drank some more and watched Barbara across the seat. "Mrs. Belmont, you're taking a huge risk pulling the trigger."

"It'll be my pleasure. Just stay out of my way."

"What do I do?"

"Grab his phone and wallet. Take his cash, wipe everything down, ditch the wallet in the dumpster, and drive away quick. No squealing tires to attract attention, but you're not dawdling either. The phone, okay? Ditch his phone so nobody ever finds it."

"Won't the police find the wallet?"

"They better. We want them to. Dead customer, money gone, wallet tossed, it looks like a robbery, amateur work. Except no prints."

"That makes sense."

"Henry's date with Marilyn didn't go too good. Instead of a kiss good night she put one in his noggin."

Barbara told Mary she needed to work on her story for when the cops came to interview her. Mary thought out loud. She kept Henry's schedule. Part of her job was knowing where he was all day.

But this day she didn't. This day there was an open spot on his schedule, and she had no idea he was going to a hotel to meet a young lady, a prostitute. He'd want to keep that quiet. Especially since Henry and Mary were involved.

She planned to admit that to the cops straight on, get it out of the way. In a political office full of young staffers who work together and drink together after hours, somebody had to know. Best to come clean up top.

Barbara liked that idea. "You're getting the hang of this."

"I have access to his computer. I can search it for Marilyn-type escorts. Plant searches so when the police sniff around, it'll add up."

The excitement burned like a bonfire between them.

"But you have to be safe, too, Mrs. Belmont. For us, for our future. The cops will be talking to you, too."

"They'll be looking for Marilyn and going in circles. Don't worry, the makeup, the disguises, it all goes into the incinerator after."

Another cop car screamed along the boulevard. Barbara watched it rip out of sight, the siren slowly dying.

"We better hit it. We'll talk alibis later. They're crucial, the final piece. And absolutely no regular phone calls. Burners only from now on."

"Got it."

"You all right? You calming down a little bit?"

"It helps to hear you talk it out, Mrs. Belmont."

"Everyone calls me Barb. And we need to give you a better name. Mary sounds like a saint or something, a regular girl out on the sidewalk, and we know that ain't right."

"I like movies, too. What about a name from the movies?"

"All the old pictures have dames with great names. Let's think of something different. Let's see, Winchester College's nickname is Green, right?"

"Yeah, the Green."

"That's no good. Red's better. I'll call you Red."

"For blood. I like that."

"Whoa, you're something else, you know that? Let's stash that hat-dance money in your safe and have some fun."

CHAPTER SIXTEEN

They caravanned away from Holy Hell. Barbara stayed tight on Mary's bumper. At a red light, Mary checked the rearview and saw the glow from Barbara's Marlboro hanging from the corner of her mouth.

No face, no eyes, just the fire of the cigarette in the darkened cab.

When the light changed, Barbara blasted her horn and Mary flipped her off and hoot-laughed and crushed the accelerator and off she went, weaving down the boulevard. Strangely, being drunk didn't help her driving.

Her mind crackled over the murder plan. She liked it. The details stacked up perfectly. Henry was going to pay.

Try to find a way out now, big man. Tick-tock.

But far back in her brain something nagged at her—Barbara insisting on doing the shooting. Why would she do that? Why take that risk when I volunteered to do it myself?

No, it's fine, that's just Barb. She's tough, she's done this before and knows what she's doing. She's been with Henry longer and has more pent-up anger. After all that time, what woman wouldn't want to pull the trigger?

They got to the house at the same time. There was a big Samsung box by the front door, Dorothy's new TV. Barbara hid by the bushes while Mary went inside. Dorothy was watching TV on the living room couch.

"About time. Supper was two hours ago." Her voice found Mary's brainstem and fried it. "I could eat a big ol' horse."

"There's leftovers in the fridge, Doe. I told you."

"You definitely did not. Do you think I'd sit here starving to death if I'd known that?"

"Did you know your TV's outside?"

"What!"

"I promised you it was coming and it's here."

"Oh! Oh, my!" Dorothy almost came out of her chair. The TV nearly got her walking again. "I heard the doorbell but didn't know who it was. I don't open up when I'm alone, especially for the UPS man. Those fellows give me the jeepers. No man should wear little shorts like that."

"Dorothy, the TV."

"For Pete's sake, go get it. I need to see it."

Mary lugged the box inside. In the commotion, Barbara tiptoed in behind her and down to Mary's bedroom. Dorothy insisted she set up the TV immediately.

"I thought you were hungry."

"Not anymore. I've waited too long for my TV already. Please, it won't take long."

Mary knifed open the box and cut the plastic straps and wrestled with the packing. She pulled everything apart and lugged it over to the TV stand and got it working. By the time she'd finished, the floor was littered with packing material.

"You'll clean up this mess later, I hope?"

"First thing in the morning, Doe."

"You should watch with me. Oh, this is so exciting. Are you sure you don't want to watch with me?"

"Tomorrow we'll have a new-TV party. How about that?"

"I can't wait. You can pick up wine cooler and some Doritos."

Mary turned the volume way up, handed Dorothy the remote, and went down to her bedroom. Barbara sat on the end of the bed with her hands covering her ears.

Mary apologized. "Once I told her about the TV, there was nothing I could do."

"How do you take it, listening to her? I'm serious, it's like torture."

"She wasn't going to quit until I got that thing set up."

"I would've throttled her a long time ago. And by throttle, I mean shoot."

Mary had the $2,200 in hat-dance money in an envelope. She tossed it to Barbara. "Henry told me to give some of this to the homeless. After tonight I'm keeping all of it."

"Good girl. What does that bring you to?"

"About a hundred and ten thousand."

"Starting to be real money."

"You know the combination. I'll keep watch in case Dorothy changes her mind again."

Barbara dragged the bureau away from the wall and punched in Henry's birthday and put the money inside. She gripped the bureau and shoved it back against the wall. Mary closed the door and grabbed Barbara around the waist.

"I'm feeling wild down to my toes, Barb."

"Me, too, Red."

"But not here. I don't want to be quiet." Mary motioned toward the main part of the house. "Miss Big Ears out there. She's going to be up watching that TV all night. What about your place? Henry's at a late meeting."

"Sure, why not. I'll text you directions. Park down the street just in case."

"I'll be along after a while. Dorothy needs to eat before bed or she'll be up all night and I'll hear about it tomorrow."

Mary ran interference to get Barbara out the door, fixed Dorothy something to eat, and started off. She caught Shea Boulevard east to the Belmonts' home.

Barbara had left the maple front doors ajar. They creaked when Mary pushed them open. Barbara called from the kitchen. Mary followed her echoing voice through a series of elegant rooms.

She put her purse on the big granite countertop, pulled out the tequila bottle, and discovered that it was empty. "How about that? I can't believe I drank the whole thing."

"You drink like a trucker and drive like an old lady."

"I'm not even slurring."

"I can fix that." Barbara opened a cabinet. "I've got plenty of wine and it's calling our names. What'll it be, white or red?"

"I don't care. Anything. Red's good."

"Believe I'll have a white Zin. It feels like a Zinny night."

They each took a sip, not talking, staring at each other. Mary came around the island, put her drink down, and snuggled up to Barbara. "You must have a more comfortable room."

Barbara threw down the rest of her drink and tossed her head to indicate the hallway to the bedrooms. The master was huge. It had a circular bed and a big picture window that looked down on the city.

In a flurry of swinging arms and legs, they shed their clothes and were getting busy when Mary, over Barbara's shoulder, spotted a collection of fur coats in the walk-in closet. "Wait, wait, just one minute. You have fur coats?" Naked, Mary pulled away and went to the closet.

"At least you're not easily distracted."

"You shouldn't have these. Nobody should be killing little animals for a coat. It's just wrong. But they are sooo beautiful."

"There's three. Chinchilla, fox fur, and Russian sable."

"I've never worn fur. In my life, ever. Would you mind?"

"Go ahead, take a swing."

The coats were of different colors and designs. Mary rubbed them up and down. The fur felt wonderful.

"These are amazing. And crazy soft."

"Pick one out and take it home. Try the Russian sable."

"I couldn't. That wouldn't be right. But really, I could. Are you sure you don't mind?"

"I said it, didn't I?"

"I'd be afraid to wear one outside. Some of those animal people are seriously crazy. How much are they worth?"

"Lots. Take whichever one you want. It's all yours."

Mary reached in and separated them on the rod and pulled out the Russian sable. There was a safe built into the wall behind the coats.

"Oh. You've got your own safe, I see."

"Henry does. It's his safe."

"Everybody's stashing cash these days."

"It's business stuff, papers mostly. Except for my necklace."

"Necklace?"

"Yeah. Ah, it's nothing, really. Just this thing I picked up." Barbara quickly changed the subject. "Put it on, put it on. I wanna see."

The sable coat was a mix of colors, light brown together with a rich darker brown and traces of red across multiple vertical folds. She ran her hands along the arms and mooned over its luxury. "I could get used to this." Mary drew in her shoulders, turned her thigh and wiggled inside it.

"Gifts from three different men."

"Are you serious?"

"I'm good at what I do."

"All of a sudden, I feel glamorous. In my whole life, I've never been glamorous. I've always wondered what it would be like to have everybody looking and wishing they were me. Now I'm the one they'll envy. What is it about fur?"

"It's magic. If you're having a sucky day, fur makes everything all right."

Mary threw up the collar and pooched her lips. "What do you think?" She batted her eyes. "What are you staring at, lady? Wish you had this coat, eh? Wish you were me, eh?"

"That's my girl. Feel better already, I'll bet."

"I think you're right. It's magic."

Barbara stepped into Mary's arms. They were both ready now but didn't get far before they heard the garage door rumble open and a car pull in.

"Damn, it's Henry." Barbara ran to the closet and grabbed a pink bathrobe and threw it on. "You need to get out of here. Fast." She pressed her palms against her cheeks and made an exaggerated horror face. "It's the walking dead!"

Laughing, Mary scurried around scooping the rest of her clothes off the floor. She had no time to put them on. With everything stacked up in her arms, she looked this way and that trying to decide what to do with them before stuffing them under the bed.

The door that led into the house from the garage opened and closed, and Henry's deep voice echoed off the tile floor. "I'm here! Meeting canceled. Thank you very much. Cocktails at Hacienda de Belmont!"

Barbara shoved Mary out of the bedroom and across the hall into a guest bedroom. She was still wearing the sable coat and nothing underneath. They heard the musical notes of Henry resetting the house alarm.

"Where're you at? I'm home! Mrs. Belmont!"

A glass clinked in the kitchen. The refrigerator's ice dispenser bumped and groaned. Barbara pulled Mary to the sliding glass door at the back of the bedroom. Mary stumbled, almost losing her balance. "I do believe I'm drunk. I must have a talk with my legs."

Barbara gave her another shove and Mary shoved back. They kissed. Mary started toward the glass door. Barbara whistled softly and handed her purse to her.

Mary pointed to the door. "What about the alarm?"

"Doesn't work on this door. The lock's broken, too. Get going."

Mary threw open the coat, made a shocked face as she flashed Barbara, who gave Mary another gentle shove. "What a tramp. Go, go, go on. Get out of here."

With one foot out the door, Mary stopped and, with a wide swing of her arm, blew a theatrical kiss and disappeared into the backyard darkness.

Henry's voice boomed down from the kitchen. "Barbara! Is that you!?"

"Of course it's me. Who else would it be?"

"I hear voices."

"I sing when I'm happy, you know that." Whispering: "How could I not be happy with you for a husband, you flabby-ass toad."

"Didn't sound like singing to me. If it was singing, it was awful."

"You expect Lada Gaga? I have a surprise for you, Henry. Are you ready?"

Barbara walked down the hall to the kitchen.

Henry pointed to the two wineglasses on the counter, one red and one white. "What's going on here? Company?"

"Couldn't make up my mind."

"Hmm." Henry sipped his bourbon.

Barbara moved close, opened her bathrobe, and rubbed against him. "Been waiting for you, sweetheart."

"Not this again."

CHAPTER SEVENTEEN

Drunk and feeling a fierce happiness, Mary drove along the broad boulevard toward home. She was naked inside the sable coat and nobody knew. None of the other drivers knew. Nobody in the whole city knew. All the secrets of the night belonged to her.

Hanging a sable arm out the window, she punched the gas pedal and sped along with one hand on the wheel, the wind battering her face and riffling her hair.

Lights flashed in her mirror and a motorcycle cop rolled alongside, motioning for her to pull over. She was opposite a city park, and as she swung into the entry lane, she heard the cop's radio squawk with a new call.

His engine revved and he roared away down the boulevard.

Mary bounced over a traffic block and crushed the brakes to send the car skidding across sand and broken glass to a sideways stop. She sat with her head against the steering wheel to catch her breath.

The close call obliterated the happiness she had felt moments earlier, and once again, the only thing on her mind was Barbara, and the murder plan.

Nothing happens the way it's planned. Something always goes wrong. There's going to be a crack-up at some point that night.

Think, think.

She opened the glove box. No tequila. She was losing her high, and if she fell off the moon entirely her mind would turn to mush. She needed a boost.

For the first time since Winchester, she wanted a cigarette. She stepped out of the Corolla and walked to a trash bin, tipped it over, and in the glow of the overhead light, picked through the scatter of junk.

She found a half-smoked butt and extracted it with her fingertips. Straightening, she startled at seeing a street dog standing beside her, his hair matted with leaves, skin burned to copper. He was wrapped neck to ankle in a filthy gray blanket. His feet were black and bare.

"Yup, yup. Looking for a ciggy."

Mary swung her arm to close the coat and conceal her nudity. "You shouldn't sneak up on people. What's wrong with you?"

"Sorry, me." His claw hand poked through the folds of the blanket. It held a lighter. He flicked it, the flame jumped, and Mary, hesitating at first, leaned in. She turned her head, hissed in a lungful, and pulled back, smelling him.

"You're a bad case, mister. You stink like I feel."

"Wanna know a secret?" His eyes were searchlights against the darkness of his skin.

"Sure. What do you got? My whole life's a secret."

Mary puffed and thought of Winchester. When she smoked there, it was with her girlfriend on the grass by the lake at night. They'd drink too much and get close and roll around and afterward lie on their backs and smoke and sing songs by Atomic Kitten while staring at the sky.

The street dog put a hand to the corner of his mouth. "Best place for ciggies." His eyes shifted from corner to corner. "The golf course, yup, yup."

Lips mashed together, he gave a conspiratorial nod. "They light up waiting on the tees. After driving they go on down chasing after their little ball and leave the ciggie squished up under the bench. If you know how to straighten 'em out, you can get yourself a good old smoke. Yup, yup."

He pulled out a Marlboro box and fingered open the flap to show his collection of half-smoked cigarettes. "I watch from the bushes, and come nighttime, I sneak onto the tees and fetch 'em up. Yup. Here, take one."

"Thanks." She lighted the second cigarette with the first. "This thing tastes like a dirty sock, too. Anything fresher than this?"

His eyes dropped to the ground. He looked hurt.

She puffed the stale butt and studied him beneath the light stanchion. He couldn't have been more than four foot ten, a pixie of a man standing in the glow of the electric moon. She liked that he was tiny, smaller than her, weaker than her.

The night had delivered to her someone more wrecked than she was. She liked that, and she liked him. He gave off something she needed, something rare in the world. Total innocence.

She asked his name, but he wouldn't say. She asked again.

"Don't remember. Nope. Men like me got no names."

"It's better that way," Mary agreed and asked if he wanted a drink. "I'm going to buy a bottle. There's a place down the street. You can ride with me."

"I quit drinking."

Mary was amused. "How about that? We have a lot in common, no names, and we both quit drinking."

His face lit up with an idea. "Say, are you hungry? I have cookies, me. Oatmeal raisin. I bought'n 'em at the store. Want one?" His hands fussed under the blanket and quickly stopped. His eyes became hooded with suspicion. "Didn't steal 'em, no way. I don't steal. It's wrong to steal even when you're hungry."

"I couldn't agree more."

They ate cookies together and smoked. Mary thought of Barbara and the question just shot out of her. "Would you murder somebody if you didn't have to?"

Street Dog didn't know what to say to that and gave a nervous laugh.

"I'm talking about somebody that needs to be dead. I wanted to do it, but this other person said, no, she was going to do it. Does that make sense to you? Volunteering to kill somebody when you don't have to?"

"I wouldn't murder nobody. That's wrong, too. Stealing, murdering, coveting, and cavorting. The Lord's watching you and now he's watching me. You shouldn't talk like that."

He looked behind him and to both sides as if expecting divine company.

"You're not leaving, are you?"

"Leaving, me. Yup, yup."

"Don't go. I need somebody to talk to." Don't you understand, there's nothing inside, no skin, no heart, no blood. Only a skeleton, a rack of bones where there should be someone real and alive. "You think I'm rich and special wearing this fancy coat, don't you? This rich lady's coat? I'm not. Look!"

She threw it open, revealing all of her naked body.

"Oh, boy. Oh, boy." Street Dog opened his blanket, and he wasn't wearing clothes either. He had mummy flesh. He wasn't embarrassed for himself or much interested in Mary. He closed his blanket. "Naked in the park, yup. Me and you. No clothes, no name."

"See, we're alike. You can talk to me and I can talk to you. Let's take a ride. I'll buy a bottle of tequila down the street."

"Places to be, me. Appointments, me. Yup, yup."

"Please. I'm asking you. This is a lonely night for me." Mary felt herself sinking. The ground was water, and if she went under, she'd never rise again. She puffed her second butt down to the filter and flicked it away.

"If you don't want tequila, I'll buy you fresh smokes. Just come with me. I can't be alone tonight. I need a stranger, someone to listen to me. Someone like you that I'll never see again.

Someone broken and miserable. You understand, right? I know you do."

Street Dog pulled the blankets tighter under his chin. "I collect ciggies, me. All the day long." His voice was singsongy.

"Look, I'll drive you wherever you want to go. Anywhere around here."

"My feet take me all over the world, to all my special places." Street Dog couldn't abide her desperation and started to back away.

"I'll buy you shoes. I'll buy you clothes and cigarettes, whatever you want." Mary was ice-cold and flailing. The dark water was up to her neck now. "Why won't you help me?"

Still backing up: "No murder for me. Nope, nope, nope."

"I can't be alone." She threw open the sable coat again. "Look at me! You don't have to fear me. Why are you afraid? I'm just like you."

"Murder's wicked, lady. I ain't like you." Waving over his shoulder as he departed: "Remember, hi-ho the golf course. Fifteenth hole. Best ciggies in town, yup."

He walked away in tiny steps on his appalling chicken feet. Mary kept pleading, holding her arms out and pleading. But the darkness swallowed him and she was alone. The sky wouldn't help. Even with her arms out, beseeching, the stars were indifferent to her misery.

She climbed into the Corolla and sped down the boulevard to the drive-through liquor store. She ordered a pack of cigarettes and a pint of tequila.

"Here, take this." She squeezed the bills into little balls and threw them at the little man behind the little window. "Keep the change and thank Henry Belmont."

The clerk gathered the bills and gave her what she asked for. "You have a lovely evening, too. Now, get lost, why don't you."

But Mary didn't move. She ripped open the cigarette pack and banged it against her index finger until one poked out. She held the cigarette but didn't light it and, as quickly as she could, twisted the cap off the tequila bottle and tipped it back to let it roll down her throat.

She lit the cigarette, drew in a lungful, and drank some more. The contentment washing over her was the best feeling she'd ever known. She leaned out the window. "What're you doing later, clerk-man? Wanna get together?"

He ignored her, pretending to be busy.

"Don't you like my fancy coat? Hey, clerk-man in the window?" She hung her arm along the side of the door, the cigarette between her fingers. She put her head back against the rest, raised her right leg, and opened the coat, showing the clerk her leg and her right breast.

The clerk slammed the window closed. Mary screamed for him to open it again, but he refused. She leaned out and spat on the window, leaving a bubbly blob rolling down the glass as she drove off laughing with the tequila bottle between her legs.

She stopped at a red light, drank more, and thought of those party nights at Winchester, and when the light turned green, she was too distracted by the pleasant memory to move. The car behind her belted its horn.

Startled and suddenly angry, Mary hung her head out the window and screamed. The car went around. She grabbed a half-filled coffee cup from the console and heaved it out the window. After that she gunned it and chased the car, blaring her own horn until her brain buffered back to the murder.

The way Barbara had sketched it out, I open the door and there she is, ready to step inside and shoot Henry. But what if that's not the plan at all? What if she's going to kill me, too, and make it look like a murder-suicide?

Then she goes to my safe, punches in Henry's birthday, and cleans me out. A hundred ten thousand dollars gone. That could sure help Belmont Construction.

With that cash she wouldn't need me. I never should've told her that combination. That money is mine. I stole it all on my own and she can't have it.

No, Mary, you're wrong. She wouldn't do that, not Barb.

But what do I really know about her? Nothing. She'd fallen deep into the criminal world, it went haywire, and she bolted.

Truth is, I don't know anything because she won't tell me. I'll fix that.

CHAPTER EIGHTEEN

At home, she crawled out of her car and dropped her keys and fumbled with them at the front door. She slipped inside and down to her bedroom before Dorothy knew she was there. She hung the fur coat in the closet, splashed water on her face, dressed in regular work clothes, and went back to the front door and banged it shut.

"Home, Doe!"

"Finally. Gosh, it's after midnight. You must've had a day for yourself."

"Busy, busy." Mary tried to walk straight but the house spiraled off the ground like in *The Wizard of Oz*. She pressed a hand against the wall to bring it back to earth.

"*The Golden Girls* is on. Come watch with me. On this new TV, it's even more hi-sterical than before."

"Aren't you hungry?"

"I'm laughing so hard I forgot to eat."

Mary made a late dinner for Dorothy and it was hard work. The house wouldn't stay still. Her hands weren't working right. She dropped a plate. It shattered and the food went everywhere.

"That's great. What's wrong with you? Is that liquor I smell?"

"I can't have a drink? How hard I work? I can't have one shitty drink?"

"You dropped my supper, does that answer your question? All day I wait for you to fix me something and you drop it and make a mess."

"I'm cleaning it up, aren't I?" Mary was practically shouting. "I don't like your language either. Talk like that, I won't tolerate it in this house."

Mary stopped and breathed and calmed herself. She wanted to get out of the kitchen and away from Dorothy. She could only think of Barbara Belmont.

"You're right, Doe. I shouldn't have said that. I do need to watch my tongue."

"It's not appropriate. I'm surprised at you."

Mary fixed a fresh plate and put it on the table. She pulled the cigarettes out of her pocket and lit one. Dorothy watched, puzzled. "You haven't smoked since school."

"Yeah, well, I've missed it."

"I thought that was over with. What's going on with you tonight?"

Mary stood with her back against the sink smoking. Her hands shook. Her whole body shook. She felt hot and dizzy. She buried her face in her hands and squeezed back tears.

With her eyes closed she could see her visitors, the people who showed up in her head when she drank. They were with her all the time at Winchester and they weren't good people. They weren't human. They weren't anything.

Their faces had no features, only blank spaces. But they spoke words, and when they were excited, they liked to dance and scream, and now they were making a terrible racket.

Barb would never do that. I can trust Barb.

Mary tossed the burning cigarette into the sink.

"If it's okay, I'll be in my bedroom. There's something I really need to do."

"Of course. You go on, then. I just hope everything's all right with you. Can you tuck me in later?"

In her bedroom, Mary took off her clothes and got into the shower with the bottle of tequila. She held it with her thumb over the spout and shoved her face against the showerhead to let the cold water pummel her. She turned away to have a sip, thumbed the spout again, and stuck her face back in the water.

Done, she stepped out, dropped the empty bottle on the bathroom floor, dried off, put on a robe, and sat on her bed and opened her laptop.

Barbara wouldn't give up the name of the mobster she was involved with but said it happened back east. That didn't narrow it down much. All those cities, New York, Philadelphia, Boston, Providence, are mobbed up. It could've been any one of them.

But one word she'd used stuck out. When Mary had ordered tequila at the Shotgun Shack, Barbara said she must really be "bullshit" at Henry. In Boston talk that meant mad. Only in Boston did "bullshit" and "mad" mean the same thing.

They have their own lingo back there.

Barbara was thirty-nine and said she'd had plastic surgery fourteen years before. Counting backwards, that meant she would've been twenty-five when she testified against the mobster and ran for her life into the magic hands of Dr. Sergio.

That told her the year of the mobster's trial.

There's a website that has every newspaper you can think of online, so you can look up stories from last week or 150 years ago.

Mary started in January of the correct year and read every issue of the *Boston Herald*. The paper is a tabloid with a liking for crime news. She figured they'd be all over the story of a big-time mobster on the hook.

She went through the winter day by day and did the same for the spring and summer, and on October 1, there it was, front-page coverage on the start of the federal trial.

Bold headlines, big photos.

You made it easy for me, Barb. You really shouldn't talk so much.

The mobster was Mickey D'Angelo, the so-called Meth King. A Massachusetts local who'd come up from the streets of Revere, he was smart, never talked on the phone. He did all his business at a lifeguard stand on the beach.

That was his office. The waves, the gulls, and the wind made him impossible to wiretap.

But the US attorney got an informant inside his circle and proved drug and murder charges against him. The judge nicked D'Angelo for thirty years. He served fewer than ten and died in prison. His henchman, Tommy Logan, the Screwdriver, got twenty years and was released after thirteen.

As far as police and prosecutors knew, Logan had never held a legitimate job. He called himself a handyman, and the nickname was because he carried a screwdriver instead of a knife. He used it for the same thing even though it made for harder work and a hell of a mess.

The Screwdriver liked to talk, liked seeing his words in print. Mary found a story about him published on his release. He said his work in the prison ministry had reformed him, and he had no intention of bringing his gang back together.

"The criminal life is nuts," he told the reporter. "I'm all done and plan to live straight from now on."

The story quoted his sister, Jennifer, saying they'd begun attending Bible study together and that Tommy had a job lined up driving a truck for a liquor distributor in South Boston. Mary tapped around and found the only one listed, O'Donnell's Spirits on D Street.

In every story about Mickey D'Angelo, the paper published his picture and that of his nemesis, too, surrounded by US Marshals as she walked into the courtroom to testify against him. The woman was Dirty Dolly Hatcher, his ex-wife.

Another picture showed their son, Danny D'Angelo. On August 31 that year, the day before Mickey's trial was to begin, Danny was killed in an accident. It was his birthday. The boy was seven.

His death pushed the start of the trial back a month, and when it finally began the media were there, swarming. The paper published a photo array that showed Dirty Dolly stepping out of a black SUV outside the courthouse.

Click. Here she is surrounded by suits walking in the door. *Click.* Here she is in a gray skirt and modest heels walking along the courthouse hall. *Click.* Here she is face forward. *Click.* From behind.

From both angles, the legs looked right.

Click, click, click. Mary studied them over and over. The body type fit. The overall shape of the face was the same, even though the features looked different. But that was Dr. Sergio's job, wasn't it, to make her look like somebody else.

Dirty Dolly Hatcher had become Barbara Belmont.

Mary brought up the main story on Tommy Logan's trial. It had a few paragraphs on Dirty Dolly. They said she was involved with another criminal before D'Angelo, a high-end jewel thief named Ricky Peel.

Born in New York, he grew up in France and did jobs around the world. He was shaggy-haired, handsome, and charming. He did stints in prison and the guards loved him. There were photos of him with the detectives who nabbed him. They were all smiling.

Cops found him dead in the backyard of his home in the upscale town of Newton, Massachusetts, at age forty-five. Cause undetermined, possible suicide. Police recovered most of the valuable pieces he'd stolen from a safety-deposit box.

But the most valuable item of all, the fabulous Dame-Burma necklace, remained missing. It was strung with exquisite Burmese rubies and valued at $2 million. Mary thought of Barbara saying she kept a necklace in her safe, and that it wasn't worth much.

So why keep it in a safe? Nobody keeps cheap jewelry in a safe. The necklace in the safe was the Dame-Burma necklace.

Mary closed the laptop and picked up the phone to call Barbara.

I might've finished second in my class, but I can figure things out better than anybody.

She punched in the number, changed her mind, and tossed the phone on the bed. The bad people were up and dancing again, and the smell of them was awful. It made her sick. She needed to do something fast to shut them up.

"Doe! Doe, do you need me!?"

"Yes, I need you. Why are you shouting down the hall? You didn't want to be disturbed, remember?"

Mary hurried out to the living room. She leaned close and held Dorothy's hand until the bad people quieted down. She helped Dorothy use the bathroom and get into bed. She kissed her on the head and said good night, and when she tried to leave Dorothy grabbed her arm and squeezed hard.

"I don't know why you can't treat me this way all the time."

"I'll try, Doe. I promise."

After that, Mary sat in front of the TV and ate leftovers. With her stomach full and the tequila wearing off, she felt low and foolish for the terrible thoughts she'd had about Barbara.

Mary Rose Cleary felt a wave of love. She called to Little Muffin and the cat jumped into her lap. She held it tight against her chest. "Barb wouldn't do those things, Little Muffin. You have to believe me. You're worried for nothing, Little Muffin."

She kissed the cat. The animal struggled against Mary's grasp, jumped to the floor, and sprinted away. Mary's heart soared as she grabbed her phone and called Barbara. "It's me. I wanted to hear your voice. I miss you so much."

"How nice."

"Where is he?"

"In bed. I'm out by the pool. You have no idea how close we came tonight." Barbara explained about the wineglasses on the counter. "I had to do some fast thinking, and I'm happy to report I've still got it."

"I read about Dolly Hatcher. I'm so sorry about little Danny. That must've been awful."

Barbara gasped, a sharp, hissing sound.

"I don't know why you couldn't tell me. You can tell me anything."

"Sometimes you can be a little too smart."

"It's not a big deal. I'm a curious person. I like putting facts together."

"You had no damn right." Barbara's words struck like a hammer blow. "I told you to drop it. Didn't I tell you to drop it and never ask me again?"

"I don't— Barb— It's nothing. I—I—I just wanted to know."

"You don't trust me, is that it?"

"No, no. Barb—please."

"When I tell you I don't want to talk about my past, I mean it. I need somebody I can trust. If we're going to go through with this, everything's gotta be square between us. No bullshit, no going behind my back."

"I get it, I understand. Absolutely. I'm sorry."

"Don't be sorry. I don't need sorry. Are you on board or not?"

"Of course I am. Nothing's changed."

"Say it again."

"Nothing's changed, Barb, I swear." Mary was going to ask about Ricky Peel and the Dame-Burma necklace but dropped that idea fast. "I need to see you. I can explain. I'm so sorry. Let's go to the Shotgun Shack right now."

"It's too late."

"When can I see you again?"

"Tomorrow's out. Board work." Board work meant her charities.

"The day after?"

"Day after, maybe. I don't know. I'll call you."

"Are you sure? You'll call me?"

"That's what I said, isn't it?"

CHAPTER NINETEEN

Next day Barbara walked through Logan Airport, picked up her rental car, and drove into the city. The smell of salt air brought the memories back. All of them right in front of her eyes, in vivid detail, in high definition.

Ricky Peel, Mickey, the horror of Danny.

The old feelings hit hard.

It was a hazy, humid afternoon. Nothing could match a Boston heat wave. The wet air clings to the back of your neck like a creature. She wanted to see some of the familiar places and drove along the beach on Columbia Road past the Farragut statue to First Street.

She took First to D Street and parked across from O'Donnell's Spirits, a prisonlike redbrick building.

What she'd seen on the way upset her. The cars were new and expensive. The people wore Beacon Hill clothes. The triple-deckers had all been renovated and nicely painted and she cringed thinking of the exquisite things the remodelers had done to the insides.

South Boston looked nothing like she remembered. Too much new money had come in and changed everything. But she had to shove that out of her mind. This was a business trip.

She waited outside O'Donnell's and watched the delivery trucks coming and going. She could see the drivers' faces when they slowed and turned off the street into the fenced parking enclosure in back.

At 6:10 p.m., she spotted Tommy Logan. She watched him park his truck and walk into the building. She gave him time to clock out, then called the office on her burner and asked to speak with him.

"It's urgent. We have a family emergency."

"Who should I say is calling?"

"Jennifer. Please, it's urgent."

"Did you say Jennifer? Is there a last name?"

"I'm Tommy's sister. I'm in the emergency room. Wait, here they are now. I'm sorry, I'm sorry, the doctors are coming. I need to speak with the doctors. Oh, my God. Have Tommy call me back."

Barbara made herself sound breathless and desperate. She cut off the call and waited. A Mercedes passed going in one direction and a Lexus in the other. Barbara stuck her middle finger out the window.

In a few minutes, her cell rang with music from *Mary Poppins*. The ploy had worked. She wanted Logan's cell number and now she had it.

"Jen? I got your message. What the hell's going on?"

"I got a job for you, Tommy."

He hesitated. "Who's this? Hey, what is this? This ain't Jen. Who's calling?"

"I need some shovel work done. Twenty thousand clams. They still dig clams around here or is that over, too?"

Long silence.

"Can I assume you're interested? Why do I even ask? I know you are."

"Who the hell's this? And, no, I ain't interested."

"That's a lot of candy for one night's work."

Another long silence.

"You're still there, Tommy. If you're not interested, why not hang up?" Barbara could hear him breathing into the phone.

"That's what I thought. Castle Island. Harborside railing, fifteen minutes."

Castle Island was just down the street. It sits on Boston Harbor at the tip of City Point. In the middle of it there's a mysterious-looking Revolutionary War fort with high granite walls and a walking path around it.

In hot weather the island fills up with picnickers lolling on the grass and people strolling the path with their babies and dogs.

Elbows on the railing, Tommy Logan watched Barbara walking toward him. He studied her in a random way, the way he studied all women. As he looked, his memory stirred, and when she got close, he stood up straight, focusing hard.

The eyes did it. His face curled behind a baleful grin. "You gotta be shitting me."

Logan had a stocky build and bowed legs. He had a wide nose with tunnel nostrils and a twisted expression on a face made for fighting. He wore baggy jeans and a gray T-shirt.

The man with him, Jimmy No Lips, had a chinless Irish face, blotchy red, narrow blue eyes, and a disappearing mouth. He might've weighed 130 pounds. He looked like a rake under a backward ball cap, spaghetti hair hanging down.

"Hello, Tommy."

"Dolly Hatcher. Well, well."

"Long time."

"Dirty Dolly. That voice has been in my head since I got the call and I couldn't place it. You don't look the same, but I could never forget them eyes."

"Don't I look lovely?"

"You always had big balls, Doll."

"You know it, the queen of the bitches."

"Big balls. Wherever you was, nobody could out-bitch you. But maybe you're pushing a little too hard right now."

"What're you gonna do, Tommy? Kill me in front of all these people?"

The crowd walked along the path. Their voices mixed with the screeching of a thousand gulls scavenging on the jetty below the railing.

"Be worth it, huh. Dreamed about it every night for thirteen years. Seen that face in my sleep, in the yard, the toilet when I was taking a leak. Everything in the hole had your face on it."

"Not anymore. Got me a new one. Why I'm alive, right?"

"For now."

"That was a long time ago and you were never the target, Mickey was. They jammed me up and you had to take a hit."

"Know how many club ears Mickey had looking for you?"

"You don't think I knew?"

"Every untied shoe in town."

"But here I am, beautiful and back in business. You can be, too."

A heavy evening breeze blew. The island sat under a flight path to the airport, and the planes flew so low it felt like you could reach up and touch them.

"I got me a job with Mr. O'Donnell. What makes you think I wanna work with you?"

"You're here and you wanna get paid. Let's not waste time, Tommy."

"Talk."

"There's two people need to be dead. My husband and his mistress."

"Did somebody get their little heart broke? Is that the problem?"

"That's my business."

"I doubt it. That'd mean you have one."

Logan scratched himself and gazed at the cargo ships on the green water. In the other direction, the sun was making its getaway, sliding down behind the dirty buildings of the old town. A plane dropping to land at Logan made talking pointless.

They stared at each other until the roar eased.

"I'm a workingman. I drive a truck and go home at night, sit around."

Barbara Belmont nodded toward Jimmy No Lips. "Is that why you have friends like this hood?"

"Hood? Jimmy? You're a hood? Is that what you are, Jimmy, a lousy hood? I should be careful around you. Don't wanna get rubbed out. You carrying a gat, Jimmy? Is that how you do your rubouts?"

They both laughed, shoulders bouncing.

"First of all, Doll, that word, it's long gone. Nobody's a hood no more. We call ourselves gents. Ain't that right, Jimmy?"

"I'm a major gentleman." He rolled his shoulders. "I give lessons on being dainty."

"You got it wrong, Doll. Jimmy here's my food taster."

Jimmy No Lips elbowed Logan. They both laughed again.

"Mickey's gone, rest his soul." Barbara looked toward heaven, but not for long. "The gang's gone, you got no money and nothing going on. Hang on to your grudge or get back in the game, that's your choice."

"Game? I don't play Parcheesi."

Jimmy squeaked out a laugh. Logan gave him a playful shove.

"You got nothing to look forward to except climbing into that rig every morning and drinking yourself blind every night."

"Could be I'm looking forward to coming to see you, Doll."

"Men have been wanting to kill me for years, and I'm still here. Try not to be a dope for five minutes."

The color in Tommy's face deepened. He hitched his pants. "It ain't polite to talk that way, not on my island. You called me, Doll. You tracked me down."

"Easy. I apologize. Don't get your feelings hurt. You're a freaking genius. Twenty grand's a lot of money."

"I'm in a bowling league, I collect coins, whatever. I'm done talking."

"Did you just say my island? What, you're the mayor? No, you're Tommy the Screwdriver Logan, and that's all you'll ever be unless you wake up."

"Take a walk, Doll."

"It's cooled off nice, maybe I will." Barbara pulled out her phone and pressed redial. Logan's phone rang in his pocket. His ringtone was Neil Diamond's "Sweet Caroline."

"Now you have my number. Call when you change your mind."

CHAPTER TWENTY

Barbara walked to her car. On Columbia Road and again on West Broadway, she saw the same set of rectangular headlights in her rearview. She laughed out loud.

"What a putz." She punched in Logan's number. "You run an amateur operation, Tommy. Mickey's up there wondering where he went wrong."

"What're you talking about?"

"The clown you got following me. Let me save you some trouble. Right now I'm gonna go pick up some doughnuts at Mae's."

"Best crullers in town."

"After that I'll get on the Southeast Expressway and head down to Milton. Got someone I need to visit. You can stay on my rear end if you like, but given the quality of your help, I doubt you can do it."

"Don't know what you're talking about."

"Should I drive slow to give your bloodhound a chance? Would GPS help?"

"You never was a comedian, Doll."

"Just to give you a heads-up, I don't know whether I'm flying out tonight or not. I don't know what shape I'll be in, so I left it open. It's a personal matter, what I got to do. But you're welcome to have your man stay with me as long as he likes."

Tommy said nothing.

"But when I do head back, it'll be first-class on account of that's the only way I fly. I can't sit back with the population. See, Tommy, that's what people do when they have money. They have choices, they buy comfort, and that's what I'm offering you. I guess we'll have to wait and see whether you're smart enough to live first-class."

"Are you a travel agent now? Is that what's going on here?"

Barbara looked in the rearview mirror at the same rectangular headlights. "With twenty Gs you could at least hire better help." She tsk-tsked. "This is sad."

Milton is the first town south of the city, a pretty suburb with tree-lined streets and beautiful homes. The town cemetery is a picturesque old New England place, graceful green hills surrounded by a low fieldstone wall.

The gates were locked by the time Barbara got there. She parked on the street along the outer wall and sat behind the wheel trying to steady her breathing. Out the window and through the sugar maple trees, she could see the tall Celtic cross on the hill.

I can't do this. I shouldn't have come here. What if he doesn't understand? What if he can't forgive me?

Barbara's breathing was shallow, the pulse in her neck thumping. She tried not to look at the cross. The last time she was here was the worst day of her life, and every moment of it was engraved on her mind.

Make a decision, Barb. You can't sit here forever. If Tommy Logan wants to, he can have five gunnies here in minutes, and there'll be no escape.

Small noises came from the darkness of the hill. No sound in a cemetery at night has a worldly origin. A child's voice calling to her. Is it him? Yes, it's him. He wants to see me. She stepped out of the car, butt-scooted over the wall, and walked up the hill and sat on the ground in front of the cross with the bag of donuts in her lap.

"I brought you these, baby. I know how much you liked having Mae's doughnuts before bed. It's almost bedtime, isn't it, my sweet. Remember?"

Barbara heard Danny's voice and saw his face. He was there, not a dream, not a wish, not an apparition, the boy himself. All this time. Her beautiful Danny. He was happy with his gift and happy she'd come.

It had been fourteen years since the day of the burial. She told him that she hadn't returned sooner because after her testimony, bad men were hunting her and it was too risky.

Out on the street, the car with the rectangular headlights pulled up behind hers. She saw Jimmy No Lips step out and stand against the grill, arms folded.

"I have to talk fast, sweetheart. There's a man there. He followed me and more might be coming. They never forget."

She described her life in Arizona. She told him she'd been successful in business and lived on the side of a mountain in a big house with a swimming pool. She talked about everything good that came into her mind.

She tried not to look at his dates etched into the cross. Seeing them would resurrect everything about that day. It would wipe her out. She fought as hard as she could but looked anyway, and it all came back.

She remembered Danny going outside to ride his bike and hearing a distant sound that turned out to be the crash, but not knowing it, and a while later a frantic banging at the door.

One of the neighbors had come for her. Some people held her back from seeing her boy or the mangled bike, but later she made the identification, and did so bravely and without tears.

She remembered the priest at the burial speaking all the right words and watching his eyes wander as he talked. Seeing that, she knew her boy would be alone in the next world. She'd vowed not to leave him alone in this one, but after fourteen years she knew she'd failed.

She explained that to Danny, why she couldn't come, and he said he understood. She thanked him and said she loved him. Again and again she said it, and he said he loved her, too.

They hugged and it was hard to let go. He asked her to return again soon, and she promised. She left the bag of doughnuts on the grave and walked down the hill to the car.

Jimmy No Lips waited, grinning stupidly, one foot crossed over the other. "What's going on, lady? Having a nice time visiting the damned?"

Barbara gave no outward reaction. But all through her body she felt a runaway rage.

"Tommy wants me to give you a message. He's in. He's gonna give you a call." He spread his hands. "We're freakin' partners."

Barbara picked up a big rock and started marching briskly back toward Jimmy.

"Whoa! Whoa, there! What're you gonna do with that, eh, lady? What do you need a rock for?"

Her furious face and determined walk told Jimmy she didn't want to talk.

"Did you hear me or what? We're working together. Hey! Hey! What—oh, shit! Feet don't fail me now!" He let out a high cackle, scampered in behind the wheel, fired the engine, and spun into a U-turn.

Before he could get away, Barbara ran after the car and heaved the rock through the rear windshield, smashing it to pieces. She almost fell on her face from the forward momentum.

Hopping on one leg: "Tell Tommy I can't fucking wait!"

CHAPTER TWENTY-ONE

Throughout that day Mary couldn't reach Barbara. She felt sick about it. She wanted to scream. She started calling when she got up in the morning, called again on the way to work, and every time Henry left the office, she fished her burner out of her purse and called again.

Barbara didn't pick up. Mary tried to concentrate on her work but couldn't.

Henry saw something wasn't right. "I know what it is."

"You do?" He knows? How could he possibly know?

Henry sat on the corner of his desk and folded his hands in his lap. Self-assured, in control. "You think old Henry Belmont isn't going to win this thing. Is that what's going on?"

"Right again, Henry."

"That's what I thought. Let me help you out. The media like a race and want to make it look close. And down the stretch they come—" He imitated an announcer calling a horse race. "So that's the kind of stories they write because they think that's what the people want. But our best minds say that's not so, that we've got this. Does that make you feel better?"

"I'm glad."

"We're going to win. I have a real good feeling."

"How nice."

He wrinkled his eyebrows. "You're not yourself tonight, Mary."

"I love you, Henry. I've told you that before. And I'll always do what's best for you. You believe that, right?"

"That's what I like to hear." He pointed at the couch. "Let's take a tumble. It'll perk us both up. I've got a backyard coffee in Scottsdale a little later, but we've got time."

If Barb is backing out, I'll do this myself. She volunteered to help and now it looks like she's backing out. Either way, Henry, you're going down.

She stared at him with flat, lifeless eyes. "Do you ever wonder how long you'll live, Henry?"

"Ha ha. You really are having a strange day. I'm talking about having some fun and you're talking death. That's a switcheroo. Rest assured, I only think that about my enemies."

"I couldn't stand it if I didn't get to Washington, Henry."

"Told you, we're going to win."

"I mean me. Living there with you, working together every day."

"What's that? Oh, yes, of course. Washington. Everything's on track. You don't have to keep bringing it up."

"Maybe I should come with you."

"What did I just say?"

"I mean to Scottsdale. To your coffee tonight."

"Oh. There's nothing for you to do. It's just rich people trying to get richer."

She studied the pumping vein in his forehead, the one that curls down across the temple like a snake. When he's dead, that vein will flatten and be still forever.

"I keep thinking about how hard it is to be a candidate, under a microscope all the time. I worry about you, that all this work is taking a toll."

"It won't be much longer, Mary."

She smiled inside. You're right about that, Henry. It won't be long at all.

"I'm going to make a few more calls, see if I can scare up some cash. Why don't you go on home and get some sleep? I'll take care of things here and tomorrow we'll start fresh."

Henry fixed himself a drink and threw darts until Mary left. She climbed into her Corolla and started for home. She pressed redial for Barbara Belmont. Straight to voice.

Where are you, Barb? Why aren't you calling back?

I have to know. Are we still on?

Mary changed directions and got onto the 101 North to Scottsdale and the Belmont home. If Barbara was there, they were going to have a serious talk. Mary had a pint bottle of tequila in the glove. She sipped as she drove.

First she lies to me about the Dame-Burma necklace, and then she disappears. Something's not right. This isn't the way it's supposed to go.

I need answers and I'm going to get them.

She rolled through the Belmonts' neighborhood of million-dollar houses. The streets were clean and perfect and the sidewalks empty. Except for lights bracketing the front door, the Belmont mansion on Eagle Dancer Drive was dark.

She circled the block and returned and parked at the curb opposite the house and studied it through the passenger window. The garage had sunburst windows. If Barbara was inside asleep, her car would be in the garage.

Mary walked across the street and cupped her hands at her eyes and looked inside. The Ford SUV wasn't in the garage, and Mary returned to her car and waited some more. Over and over she hit redial on Barbara's number. No answer.

She knew she had had too much to drink, but it still wasn't enough. She sat there sipping from her bottle and staring at the house. No strange car sits in that neighborhood for long without getting noticed.

After thirty minutes she gave up and drove home. She fed Dorothy and wheeled her into her bedroom. Every night it was the same thing. Shake out her medicine, wrestle her into her nightclothes, and lay her down on her back in bed.

"There. All set. You have a good night."

"Why am I smelling liquor again?"

Mary had thought it was over until the morning. "Can't you just let it go for one night?"

"You're back to your old ways. Smoking and drinking. We talked about how things go bad for you when you do this."

"Good night, Doe. I hope you don't have terrible dreams with monsters chasing you."

"What kind of thing is that to say?"

"You told me that's what you dream about. You said so yourself."

"So you have to remind me?"

"If you don't want me to mention your monsters, don't talk about them. Night-night, Doe."

"Such a thing to say to a person."

In her bedroom, Mary sat on the bed sipping from her bottle. She couldn't get her mind off the Dame-Burma necklace. She Googled it. No authenticated photo existed. All that came up was an artist's full-color rendering.

Burmese rubies have a red-blue color, and there was light inside the stones, the smallest bits of winking light. There were maybe thirty of them, each set in a small silver heart circled by brilliant white diamonds.

An accompanying story said it had once been owned by France's empress Joséphine Bonaparte. Mary knew all about Joséphine, had read everything about her at Winchester. She loved diamonds and jewels, loved to show them off.

After she and Napoléon divorced, all her jewels were stolen. To allay suspicion that he'd committed the robbery and preserve his reputation, Napoléon hired a famous jewel thief to find them, and he did.

Except for the Dame-Burma necklace.

From the early nineteenth century on, it traveled the world in the hands of one illegitimate owner after another. One of the stories Mary read included a map tracing its journey through several world capitals, until it fell into the hands of a retired MI6 agent.

He lived in a modest London apartment on the Thames. Some sources said Ricky Peel had stolen it from there. Mary read for an hour. Many betrayals and murders had occurred in its wake.

Reading about it excited her, the necklace excited her, and she was sure that Barbara had it. She remembered Barbara's reaction when she found out the combination to Mary's safe was Henry's birthday, her rolling laughter.

"Sometimes you can't make it up." That's what Barbara had said.

Mary had thought that odd at the time but let it go. Now it slapped her in the face—what if Henry's safe had the same combination? Mary had to know if she was right.

Henry was at his coffee and Mary knew how to get into the Belmont house without setting off the alarm.

You poked around my house, Barb, and now I'll poke around yours.

After making sure Dorothy was asleep, she got in her car and drove to Scottsdale.

CHAPTER TWENTY-TWO

Just past 11:00 p.m. and this time the house was lit up. There were two cars in the driveway, Henry's and another, not Barbara's. The second one was a red Porsche with the top down.

Mary slipped into the darkness at the side of the house and along the narrow space between the bougainvillea and the garage. She heard sounds in the backyard.

Henry's voice, a woman giggling, Henry's laughter, water splashing.

Mary reached the gate she'd escaped through before. Peering over, she saw Henry floating in the pool, and there was Sherry Waterman from the Boys Home, her legs in the water toeing Henry's raft. Both held drinks and both were naked.

Barbara lied to me and so did you, Henry. That's what this world is, a paradise of liars.

Getting into the house could be a problem. There were two back doors. The farthest one from Mary entered the kitchen, and the closer one, with the busted alarm, went into the guest bedroom.

If they got distracted enough, maybe she could slip along the rear of the house and in that bedroom door without being seen. She'd have to be fast and completely quiet.

Sherry got into the water and pushed Henry around in his raft. They were laughing. She took Henry's hand in two of hers and leaned back and pulled him around in circles.

"Wheee!"

He jerked her close and they kissed.

Now was the time. The latch on the gate rattled when Mary lifted it. It jarred her and she stopped, waiting, but their frolicking covered the sound. Carefully, she pushed the gate open a few inches and the hinge squealed.

"Did you hear that?" Sherry Waterman bent her neck toward the sound.

"Hear what?"

"That noise."

"Wind. Probably wind."

"That didn't sound like wind, Henry."

"There's always wind off the mountain."

"Go check. Will you go check?"

"I'm not gonna check. You check."

"The man's supposed to check. What's wrong with you? That's a rule."

"I'm comfortable floating here. I'm cozy as hell. There's all kinds of noises around here at night, different things. I'm sure it's nothing."

"People get massacred in big spooky houses all the time. You need to check. Where's your wife at, anyway? You never said."

"Out of town. Don't know where and don't care. You wanna go check, so check. Nobody's stopping you."

"All right, I'll check. You're such a douche."

Sherry climbed out of the pool. She was put together, blond, tall. On her toes, she walked toward the gate, naked, dripping, shivering, arms folded against her chest.

With her coming closer, Mary jumped behind the bushes. She got down on her heels, making herself as small as she could, and lowered her face so that her eyes wouldn't catch a sliver of starlight and give her away.

She didn't dare breathe.

Sherry found the gate ajar and pulled it shut with a loud clank. "This was open, Henry. Over here, your gate, it was open."

"I told you it was the wind. Javier can oil the hinges."

"Have him fix your door lock, too. On the guest bedroom."

"I'll have Mary call him. Hinges, door lock, anything else?"

"Call him yourself. Pick up the phone and call. It's your house. You use that chick for everything."

"Get back here, will you? Purple-helmet boy is leaving town."

"Oooh, we can't have that."

When she reached the pool, Henry pulled her into the water. She screeched and locked her legs around his middle and he twirled her about.

Mary decided she couldn't get inside the house with them in the pool. She waited in the bushes, not moving, sweating in the night heat. Twenty minutes later, Henry and Sherry climbed out of the pool and put on their robes and went into the kitchen through the sliding glass door.

When Mary heard the latch catch, locking the door, she opened the gate enough to squeeze through and tiptoed along the deck to the guest bedroom and slipped through the door. She waited, listening. The sounds from the kitchen told her that Henry and Sherry were freshening their drinks.

Mary darted across the hall into the master bedroom, spread the fur coats out along the rod, and punched at the keypad on the safe. She pulled on the door and it opened.

Henry's birthday. Right again. Mary felt the pride well up inside her.

There it was, the Dame-Burma necklace, an exact match to the online image. She laid it across her hand and felt a thrill. More than 220 years missing and now it filled her palm and dangled from her fingers.

She stared and stared until the voices in the kitchen changed and she heard sounds of movement.

Mary put the necklace back in the safe, shut the door, and jumped across to the guest bedroom just as Henry and Sherry skipped down the hall, grabbing each other, bumping against the walls, and spilling their drinks as they went. They hopped into bed.

Mary could've let herself out the door and gone home. Instead, she waited, listening. She didn't want to leave.

You should know someone has been here, Henry. Someone has been in your house. I want you to think about that and know that whoever it was came in at night, in the dark, and can do it again anytime.

She crept out of the bedroom and down to the kitchen. In the cabinet she got out two wineglasses and put them on the counter. She got out the bottle of white Zinfandel and the bottle of red, the same ones she and Barbara had drunk from.

She poured three fingers of white Zin into one glass and three fingers of red into the other and left them on the granite countertop. As she put the bottles away, she bumped the bottom cabinet, and the sounds in the master bedroom stopped.

The house fell silent for a long moment, and then Henry's questioning voice started up, low at first but becoming louder. The voice came closer.

Mary hopped into the adjoining dining room and hid in the crook between the wall and a big hutch. On top of it sat a collection of decorative crystal, fancy dishware, silver serving platters, and several colorful Indian pots.

There was a wide middle drawer open an inch. She slipped her index finger into the crack and opened it wider, revealing an array of silverware and kitchen knives, including a black-handled carving knife, twelve inches long.

Slowly, using her fingertips for maximum quiet, Mary picked it up and held it tight at her shoulder. This time it was Henry hearing things. He reached the kitchen first.

"What the hell's this?" He pointed to the wineglasses on the counter. "Am I drunk? Were these here a minute ago?"

Sherry came up behind him and wrapped her arms around him. "Your fancy mansion is haunted. Told you."

"I'm not that drunk."

"You most certainly are, Senator."

"Not yet. Don't spook it."

He went to the kitchen door and rattled the handle. Locked. He rattled it again and checked the alarm. It was set. Cupping his hands to the glass, he peered into the backyard, saw nothing but the shimmering water, and turned to face the kitchen again, listening, thinking.

"Do you remember having wine?"

"I'm not good at remembering, like, beverages. Let's go to bed, Henry."

"But we weren't drinking wine. That's the thing. It's exactly like the other night. I know I've had a few drinks, but this is weird."

"What's like the other night?"

"The wineglasses. Right here on the counter."

"I don't know what you're talking about."

"I'm going to walk around. Something's not right."

Mary fanned her fingers on the knife handle, getting a better grip. The bad people were dancing, and the smell was unbearable.

Better stay where you are, Henry. Don't make me do this. Don't make me kill you and Sherry, too. That wouldn't be fair. Barb and I have a plan, and we're so looking forward to carrying it out.

Sherry picked up the white Zinfandel and drained it in one swallow. She did the same with the red.

"I was already mucho drunko, so that should speed things up. I figure you got fifteen minutes before I fall down and can't get up. Like one of those old ladies on TV." She machine-gun laughed. "That means no sex for you, Senator, unless you're a sicko, or whatever. So, what's it gonna be?"

That got Henry's attention, and the two of them went back to the bedroom. Mary came out of her hiding place and put the carving knife on the counter beside the two wineglasses.

"For luck," she whispered, and tiptoed down the hall. She stopped outside the master bedroom to listen. Henry and the naked woman sounded like zoo animals playing in mud.

Mary grinned and slipped out the guest bedroom door.

CHAPTER TWENTY-THREE

Barbara's plane landed in Phoenix late the next morning. Walking through the terminal, she checked her burner and found multiple text messages from Mary.

The first few were declarations of love and desperate pleas to meet. The last one was angry: "Where are you? Where *are* you? Are you backing out, Barb? Don't you love me, Barb?"

Barbara texted back: "Busy. Meet tonight for sure. Breathe."

She Ubered to work and spent the remainder of the day bouncing from the office to a job site in Gilbert and back again. She had meetings throughout the day. She studied blueprints. She worked hard.

Everything had to be normal. The killing time neared.

When she arrived home that night, she found Henry sitting at the center island eating Chinese takeout with a fork and drinking a Heineken. The TV was on. He chewed and pointed at the screen. "You won't believe the story they just did. They mentioned Vin the Chin."

"There you go, Henry. Any publicity's good after CBS, right?"

"Only it wasn't about me. This mob guy just died in Scottsdale. He was some big deal with the Genovese crime family. Worked for Vin the Chin Gigante. I didn't know that name. Did you know that name?"

"His crew worked out of Sullivan Street in the Village."

"Maybe it's not such a good idea, having me associated with some mobster. There's tons of people from New York out here now.'"

"Don't worry, Henry. This is Arizona. People come here to forget."

He sipped his Heineken. "Look at this now. Another dumb story."

The Phoenix station had jumped to a live remote. The anchors were banging away about a serial shooter in Maryvale, in west Phoenix. The cops had run his car off the road and he rabbited, and now they had him cornered in an abandoned building.

"Nobody's even dead. It's just noise and lights." Henry shook his head. "Look at the banner. Breaking news! Are you telling me it's more important than my Senate campaign?"

"It is to the station."

"More important than the future of this state?"

"Don't you mean the future of Henry Belmont?"

"Okay. But it has to start somewhere."

"These TV creatures don't look ahead. It's about tonight. Ratings, Henry."

"Shootings like this happen all the time in Maryvale."

"This one has a hook. Don't you want to see what's going to happen next?"

"It's all bullshit."

"Of course it's bullshit. It's TV news."

They stared at the screen, Barbara with her elbows on the counter next to Henry, who was hunched over his supper. The reporter stood in front of the crime tape for a standup. He kept looking over his shoulder to point at nothing and repeating the same set of facts.

Barbara went to the wine cabinet over the sink, grabbed a bottle, and poured a glass. Her phone buzzed with a text. The phone was in her purse on the center island next to Henry.

It buzzed again. Barbara figured the text was from Mary, but she didn't want Henry to see it. He turned toward the sound. Barbara thought of hurrying over and grabbing the phone but stopped herself. That would raise his suspicion.

"Do you want another beer? Let me get you another Heineken."

"I'm good."

The phone buzzed again. Henry looked at the purse again. "Somebody's trying to get hold of you."

"It's just work. I'm not worried about it."

He pulled the purse closer and was about to reach inside. By then, Barbara had gotten a Heineken out of the refrigerator. She shoved the bottle down the long surface of the granite island. Henry could let it crash to the floor or catch it. He caught it just in time.

"Whoa. I said I didn't want one."

"It'll help you enjoy the show." Barbara walked casually back to the island and reached into her purse to stop the buzzing. It was Mary all right. Barbara pulled a cigarette out, lit up, and pointed to the TV.

"You watch. Pretty soon they'll bring in the news chopper to ramp up the drama." Immediately after she said it, the sound started, the *whoop-whoop-whoop* of the Action News chopper. "What'd I tell you? Listen to the sound of those blades. Don't you feel the suspense?"

"This is driving me nuts. Honest to God, I'm going to have a stroke."

"You're still ticked off about CBS."

"I hate reporters."

"Everybody hates reporters. You've just had a rough few days is all."

He squeezed the cap off the Heineken and sipped. "That reminds me, have you noticed anything funny going on around here?"

"You're the one who's been home, not me."

"Where were you, anyway?"

"Conference. How many times, Henry? You don't listen."

"You weren't gone long."

"Somebody's got to take care of the business." Barbara puffed her cigarette and sipped her wine. "Funny, like ha ha?"

"Funny like, 'Oh, shit, somebody's been in here.' I mean our house."

"The wineglasses again?"

"Swear to God."

"Told you that was me. I poured two glasses and forgot. I was, shall we say, under the weather."

"Nobody was more shitfaced last night than me."

He kept eating and watching the news. Barbara pretended to watch along with him. She reached into her purse, keeping her hands hidden inside, and checked her burner again for text messages. Mary had sent several more, the panic mounting in each one.

Barbara needed to calm her down before she flipped out entirely. She was about to go out to the backyard to call when Henry turned off the TV and ditched his dishes in the sink. He had a meeting and headed upstairs to change.

When he did, Barbara went into the living room and sat on the couch and called Mary. As soon as she heard Barbara's voice, she jumped in with a jumble of excited words.

Flipping through the channels as she listened, the phone in one hand, wineglass in the other, Barbara let her run down until she stopped. "I had board work. I couldn't get away."

"For one phone call? For one minute? Two whole days?"

"I didn't want to call and put you on the spot, you know, if Henry was around. We have to be extra careful now."

"Where were you all this time?"

"Conference, charity stuff. At the Biltmore. Right down the street, actually."

The Biltmore. Henry had said Barbara was out of town. Another lie. Rather than fueling Mary's anger, it calmed her. Questions had been answered.

"It's been one thing after another. If I could've gotten away, I would've. Believe me, I missed you so, so much." Barbara sipped her wine and flipped channels as she talked. She waved good-bye to Henry as he came down the stairs and went out the front door.

"You haven't told me, are we still on?"

"Did you patch it up with Henry like I said? Apologize for kicking his ass on the sidewalk?" Barbara laughed at the memory. "Because I don't want him suspecting one tiny little thing."

"He sat me down and said he was so sorry, blah, blah. He said I was overworked."

"It's always somebody else's fault with him."

"He never brought up Monica and she's acting like it never happened."

"Beeyotch." Barbara stopped on *The Real Housewives of New Jersey*. She watched a hair-pulling fight that she hadn't seen before. It was a wild one. "Let's meet tonight. This is the last time. I mean before. We have a lot to talk about."

"When are we doing this? I need to know. It's all I think about."

"Not on the phone."

"I need to blow off steam. Let's go shooting."

"Okay, but give me an hour. I want to shower and do my makeup first. I'm gonna look like a beauty queen for you. I want to put on a show for you."

"Barb, I'm sorry I freaked. You can't know how excited I am to see you."

"Me, too."

Mary hung up and smiled to herself. Barbara hung up, tossed her phone on the couch, and yawned. She didn't realize how far behind she was on *Housewives*. She set the TV to tape so she wouldn't miss any more hair-pulling fights. She loved those.

She went upstairs to dress.

CHAPTER TWENTY-FOUR

arbara drove north on the 101 to Bell Road and the Holy Hell Gun Range. Mary was already there. She had on a vintage red boho pullover with green and white flowers embroidered on the front. Low-cut, loose-fitting, and untucked. Skinny black jeans hugged her legs down to black Chelsea boots.

She was heavily made up. Her face was paper smooth and very white. Red velvet lipstick made it seem whiter still. Liberal use of mascara had given her long, curling eyelashes.

Barbara took the lane adjoining Mary's. "Gotta say, you look swaggy tonight. Never seen you look so beautiful."

"Do you really mean it, Barb?"

"I'm going blind over here. That Glock makes a nice accessory and the Dior pulls it all together. Love that .45-caliber perfume."

"When you said you were going to dress up, I had to keep up."

"You got it going on, girl."

Barbara took off her black sunglasses. She unzipped her hoodie, pulled it off, and laid it over the counter. She worked slowly and deliberately, knowing Mary was watching through the drifting gun smoke.

She wore a black T-shirt with *Snacking for Two* across the front. She was packed into it. She had on tight jeans with the cuffs turned up. Gold ankle bracelets made the bare portion of her legs sparkle. Her pumps were black suede, her hair color for the evening a daring honey brown.

Mary studied her every move. "And here I was thinking I looked good."

"You and me together, sugar, we'd own any club in Scottsdale."

Barbara retrieved the Colt King Cobra from her purse. She reached over and touched Mary's arm. Mary took Barbara's hand and squeezed, and Barbara squeezed back. They exchanged no words for thirty minutes after that.

All they did was shoot, reloading multiple times and secretly eyeing each other's accuracy.

When she finished, Mary pulled her earmuffs down onto her shoulders and laid the Glock down on the counter between them. Barbara picked it up and removed the empty magazine. The move surprised Mary. Handling someone else's gun crossed a boundary.

What are you doing, Barb? You said you were at the Biltmore and I know you weren't. Are you playing me now?

One by one, Barbara fished bullets out of Mary's cartridge box and thumbed them into the magazine. Mary watched, then picked up Barbara's Colt and did the same, taking rounds from Barbara's cartridge box and sliding them into the Cobra's open cylinder.

The sweat on her fingers made it hard to grip the shells. But she kept going, matching Barbara's stare. Their eyes locked, and in them was a searing light that held all the excitement and danger of what was to come.

Loading each other's guns felt as intimate as anything they'd done.

"I'm going to be at a fundraiser at La Posada in Paradise Valley. Place is enormous, huge grounds, loads of people moving around, indoors, outdoors, everywhere. I can slip away, change into my Marilyn outfit in the car. Do the makeup there, too."

Done reloading, Barbara shoved the magazine into the well and handed the Glock to Mary, grip first.

"On my way back, I'll change back into my regular clothes in the car and I'll be cruising around La Posada again like I never left. 'Hello there, Mrs. Kingston, so nice to see you again.' Nobody will miss me. Nobody will know nothing."

Mary finished loading Barbara's gun, snapped the cylinder in place, and handed it over. Their hands touched and Mary felt a chill race up her back. For an instant she wished they could be alone together right then, somewhere, anywhere.

No, don't fall for it, Mary. Don't you be weak. She lied, remember? Twice. Why lie if she's not running a hustle?

"You're going to have a tight window for your alibi."

"Let me worry about that. What about you?"

"Fat Frankie Santiago. I've got him dangling on a string and Tuesday night I'll pull it."

"What is it with you and men? They lose their minds."

"It's because I don't care."

"That's it? Indifference is your big secret?"

"They can't take it and need to do something about it."

"Like a conquering thing?" Barbara nodded slowly, thinking. "I get that. Tony, my cop, he's that way. I let him think it, anyway. You cared about Henry for a while."

"That was a mixed-up time and it's over now. Being around you has taught me how wrong I was. Whatever, he's about to be past tense."

"My favorite tense."

They went back to shooting. James Madison, the range manager, opened the door separating the check-in lobby from the shooting lanes. "We got a car alarm screaming in the parking lot. There's only two cars out there, so it's one of ya's."

Mary paid no attention. Barbara looked away, shielding her face.

"One of you ladies needs to see what gives. The kind of jaspers we get around here, you better have a look."

Never looking directly at him, Barbara put on her black sunglasses and the hoodie and grabbed her keys and hurried out. Madison stayed put, back against the open door, legs straddling both rooms.

He nodded the all clear to Mary, who reached into Barbara's purse, grabbed her burner phone, and pressed the wake-up button to activate the sign-in pad.

She figured she'd have time for one try to hit on Barbara's passcode and knew what it was going to be. Mary remembered Barbara's emotional reaction when she'd mentioned Danny, and she remembered that he'd died on his birthday, the day before the first trial date.

Madison, standing in the doorway, his head turning back and forth between the door to the street and Mary, rotated his finger to her in a hurry-up signal. Mary typed in the month, date and year of Danny's birthday and the phone opened.

She felt a wave of satisfaction.

Ha! Made the right call again.

She punched up Barbara's list of calls. The most recent went to Mary's number, but the one before that was to the 617 area code. Massachusetts. Tommy Logan, the Screwdriver, lived in Massachusetts.

Madison whistled. Mary shot him a fast look. He made a rapid throat-cutting motion.

"I'm hurrying, I'm hurrying."

She memorized the number and dropped the phone in the purse. Barbara came back into the building and through the door to the shooting lanes. Passing Madison, she kept her head down so he couldn't get a good look.

"I don't know what that was about."

"Everything okay out there?"

"Alarms don't go off for nothing. With what we're doing, it makes me nervous, stuff like that happening."

"Probably just kids messing around."

"There weren't any kids out there."

"They run pretty fast."

They talked over their plan, repeating everything again. Barbara had chosen the location, the Beautiful Day Motel. It was on Fifty-First Avenue just north of the 10 along the Grand Canal.

"Thursday night."

"Thursday night."

Thursday was two days away.

"We can't meet between now and then."

Mary nodded. "That's the hard part. I really miss you. It's been so long."

Barbara held up her burner. "I'm going to toss this thing beforehand and you need to do the same. Anything else?"

"I'm so excited, Barb. This is it."

"I have to get going. Think hard. If there's anything else, now's the time."

Mary's eyes were drifting. She had a dreamy expression.

"Something's on your mind." Barbara was packing her gun away in her purse. "You're going to toss your phone, right?"

"Yeah, I will, I will. I was just thinking."

"About what?"

"What do you say to someone before a murder? I don't know what to say. I guess I'll just wish you good luck."

"Do everything like we planned and we won't need luck. The most important thing is to keep your head because it's going to get nervy."

Barbara left. They didn't hug. They didn't say good-bye. Mary gave it a few minutes and went to the front room and looked out at the parking lot to make sure Barbara had left. She handed Madison five $20 bills.

"Between us, right?"

He nodded. "Glad to do it." He licked his lips and folded the bills.

Mary stepped closer, pushing her face against his. "That's not an answer. I need to hear you say it. Is it between us?"

"Yes, yes, between us. Ma'am, I swear."

Fearing what she might find, Mary didn't call the 617 number right away. She waited until she got home and called from her bedroom. The ID window said *Anonymous*. It rang until the message came on: "This is Tommy. Figure it out."

Mary's stomach turned over. The breath left her.

Wait, Wait. Tommy could be anyone named Thomas. It didn't have to be Tommy Logan. There were a million Thomases in Massachusetts and they all went by Tommy.

No, that's too much of a coincidence. Don't be a fool, it's him.

Why would Barbara go back to the Screwdriver? Her testimony put him away for thirteen years. Would Logan work with his betrayer? Of course he would, if the money was right. Why else would she call him? Why lie about where she'd been the previous two days?

Because she'd gone to Boston to set up another betrayal.

"Barbara's going to kill me and steal my money. Did you hear that, Little Muffin?" The cat curled up in Mary's lap and purred. "She hired a bad man to shoot me dead. You were right all along, Little Muffin. I should've listened to you. Now you know what I have to do, don't you? Yes, you do. You always know."

From underneath her bed, Mary pulled out a cardboard box. She reached inside and removed a black waist band with an attached drop garter that hung down five inches to a black Lycra holster. The holster held a .380 pistol, compact but powerful.

She took off all her clothes. She secured the band around her waist and Velcroed the holster around the inside of her left thigh. At the closet, she selected a dress, black and dotted with pink circles, the hem knee-length, pockets on each hip.

She raised her arms and shook it on over her shoulders and down along her body. She grabbed the skirt at both thighs and pulled down, wiggling to get the fit right and keep the gun from printing against the fabric.

With the gun invisible, she stared at herself in the bathroom mirror, and her eyes stared back, bright and confident behind her pancaked white face. The black eyeliner extended just beyond the sockets, giving her cat eyes.

She loved the look. It made her feel powerful.

As quickly as she could, muscles tense, predator eyes squinting, Mary grabbed the skirt with her left hand, lifted it above her waist, dropped into a crouch, and jerked the pistol out. She did that over and over, arms extended, double-gripping the .380 and making wet gunfire sounds as she pretended to shoot.

Satisfied that she was fast enough, she raised her left leg and planted her foot on the counter and pulled her skirt back, revealing everything all the way up. The black holster and gun stood out against her creamy white thigh. She grinned into the mirror.

"Hello there, Barb. I believe you're right. I am beautiful."

CHAPTER TWENTY-FIVE

Wednesday. The day proceeded as campaign days do.

Too much coffee. The constant chirp and buzz of phones. That frantic energy, that pasted-on smile. Appearances, interviews, lights, makeup. Talking points updated, memorized, practiced. Henry's eager young staffers swarming, the men weevils in khakis, the women all size fours. Race to the next stop. Shake the mayor's hand. Shake everybody's hand. Purell. Wave, smile, don't flub your opening joke.

Be cool, baby.

Later, exhausted, back in the office, Henry poured himself a Dewar's, no ice. When you made calls begging for money, you couldn't have the people on the other end hearing the clink of ice cubes. They'd think you were a party boy, a lightweight.

He sat at his desk and punched in a number. He always opened the same way: "John, it's been too long. Was it something I said?"

He bellowed in laughter and put on his serious voice: "This country is in a pickle, and with your help and the help of folks like yourself, folks with vision and big American hearts, why, I know we can fix it. This is in our hands, John."

He was good on the phone. There was only his voice and his voice came down from the mountaintop. It plowed into your head and was hard to resist. Up close and in person, the attention went to his eyes, and there was something not quite right in them, a vacancy.

But in person or on the phone, he could close. Like an animal on prey.

After making his calls, he ordered Jimmy John's for the three of them. Barbara was there. She and Henry had a joint appearance later that evening. He'd asked her to introduce him to a small group of wealthy female investors.

He thought having a female do it would encourage more check writing. It wouldn't hurt to appear to be a happy couple. Barbara agreed as long as she didn't have to stay for the speech.

She wanted him happy and unsuspecting for what was to come, but she had limits. She planned to leave after the introduction, pick up Mexican from Taco Bandito on the way home, and have it laid out for him when he got there.

As they were eating sandwiches in the office, Mary waited for just the right moment before asking Henry about meeting the union man in a motel room.

This was crucial. If he didn't go for it, the plot would collapse.

"Motel room, no, no. That means I can't get up and leave easy and can't get rid of him easy. He can chew on me forever. I don't like that."

"He's got important things he wants to go over with you."

"I'm sure he does. They all do. Can't you find some quiet place? Even a rest area on the highway somewhere?"

"He insisted on a hotel."

"Insisted? See, that sounds off to me. Doesn't it sound off to you? I don't like this."

Barbara raised her eyes and peered at Mary over her sandwich. Their eyes locked. Mary gave the slightest of nods.

"He wants it real private, Henry."

"You know this guy?"

"No. Not really." As soon as that was out, Mary knew she'd made a mistake.

"Not really? Either you do or you don't."

"It's not that simple. You know, I—I meet a lot of people."

"Mary, you know him, yes or no?"

"It's fifty thousand dollars, Henry." She was boxed in and reeling and she'd grabbed the number out of the air.

Barbara pretended to choke on her food. Henry Belmont stopped chewing. "Fifty thou? I like the sound of that. Fifty thou. Jesus, somebody's looking out for me. All right, go ahead and set it up."

"One more thing, can we take two cars? You don't mind driving, do you?"

"Why would I drive? We're going together. Why can't you drive?"

"It'll be late and I've got to get back to Dorothy. She hasn't been feeling too hot lately."

"So we'll keep it short."

"It's just that afterward I have to drive you back here and it's the opposite way for me to get home. And I have to pick up her prescriptions, too."

"This whole thing, I don't know."

"I'm just worried about her, Henry, the way she's been feeling."

"Have you taken her to a doctor?"

"If anything happened. I wouldn't know what to do without her."

"You'd have a much easier life is what you'd do. I have my way of doing things, Mary." He paused and thought it over.

Mary waited. Come on, Henry. Just say yes. Say yes.

"All right, but just this one time, if you're so worried."

The three of them left the office at the same time. Henry and Barbara headed to their appearance, and Mary drove home. Dorothy had fallen asleep in front of the TV. The noise of Mary coming in startled her awake.

"Oh, my God, you scared me." She yelped and sat up. "What happened? Was I—asleep?"

"You were dreaming, Doe."

Breathing hard, confused. "I don't—I was running, so shaken up, trying to get away—from something."

"Monsters again?"

"I shouldn't sleep on an empty stomach. I'm glad you're home."

"I'll fix your supper right now. My apologies."

"My mother used to say, never sleep on an empty stomach or you'll have a fitful rest."

Mary got Dorothy fed and put to bed. She was as polite as could be. She didn't want any distractions. With the excitement surging through her body, she went into her bedroom, opened the safe, and emptied it, stuffing the cash into a shoulder sack.

Mary knew that Barbara's plan for taking her out centered around the money. She needed a place to store it until the deed was done.

After half an hour, certain Dorothy was asleep, Mary sneaked into her room and grabbed the keys to her Prius off the dresser.

The Corolla could stay in the driveway. With what Mary had planned, the Prius was better. Quieter, and unlike the Corolla, she had never driven it to the Belmont house, so it couldn't be easily linked to her if it were spotted.

In the garage she opened the hatchback, lifted the lid on the spare-tire well, removed the tire, and dropped the money sack in the hole. On a shelf in the garage she had plastic drop cloths from Home Depot. She put them over the money, closed the hatch, backed out of the garage, and headed toward Scottsdale.

Mary had two final details to square up.

Driving along, she called Fat Frankie.

"Good evening, Mr. Santiago."

He paused, trying to place the voice. "Mary? Is that you?"

"I've been thinking a lot about you. About us. It's time."

"No fooling? I thought we'd never get together. Well, well."

"You wore a nice shirt last time. I like that. It showed respect."

"That's why I wore it, you bet. Just for you. Uh-huh."

"But you didn't wear socks with your loafers."

"Huh? Socks? My feet get hot. What, that's bad?"

"Where I come from, a gentleman wears socks. If we're going to do this, you need to wear socks."

"Mary, it's summer, for crying out loud."

"You're not listening to me. I need socks. I demand socks. Do you understand me?"

"Yeah, sure, I understand. You sound different, Mary."

"You need to be clean. I need you to shower and shave and your clothes need to be fresh and clean. But the most important thing is the socks."

"Sure, yeah, socks. I got clean ones in my drawer. Anything else?"

"Tomorrow night, a few minutes either side of eight, I'll give you a call."

"Why don't I just give you the address to my Cave Creek hideaway right now? We can set a time and meet up there. Done and done."

"We're not going to Cave Creek. This is my show. Okay? I want to be clear about that."

"Oh. Oh. Whatever you say, Miss Cleary." His tone was teasing. He'd waited a long time and was happy to play whatever game she wanted. "Can I ask where we're going?"

"You'll find out."

"A mystery, eh? I like that. Okay, fine."

"Nobody can know about this, Frankie. You can't tell a single living soul."

"I can keep a secret. You wouldn't believe the stuff I hear at the restaurants."

It was a warm night, low clouds, the air still and not a sound on Eagle Dancer Drive. Mary parked down from the Belmont mansion, in the darkness between the streetlamps. She waited to make sure no one was around and walked up the winding entryway and into the darkened area beside the house.

She passed through the side gate. The hinge squealed as before. She walked along the back of the house to the bedroom door. It slid right open. She knew it would. Henry had asked her to call Javier and have him fix the lock, but she'd let that little task slip from her schedule.

You need to take care of these chores yourself, Henry. Some people you just can't trust.

She slipped across the hall into the master, opened Henry's safe, removed the Dame-Burma necklace, and closed the door. She wiped the safe down, got back to her car, and drove off.

Stopping at the first intersection, she flipped on the overhead light, took the necklace out, and studied it, mesmerized. She'd never seen a more beautiful piece of jewelry.

"I'll take good care of this for you, Joséphine. I promise." She stared, transfixed. "I have two million dollars here in my hand and all my cash in the trunk. How do you like that, Barb?"

She had one more stop to make before the night was through.

CHAPTER TWENTY-SIX

"I'm not going to say a word until I know all of you are finished with your dessert. I see a couple of stragglers out there and nobody should rush when it comes to blueberry lavender cheesecake. That's an actual law. Or it will be after Henry wins this election, if I have anything to say about it."

Easy laughter rolled through the crowd.

"So, please take your time."

The Pink Canyon Restaurant was at the end of a winding mountain road on the edge of Scottsdale. There was an L-shaped bar inside the front door. The stools were shaped like saddles. After that came the restaurant's main seating area and out back a lantern-lit patio on the edge of a cliff overlooking the city.

The heat of the day had stuck around, as usual, but misters kept people from falling over. There might've been thirty women in the audience, dressed up all the way, in the finest clothes, in sparkling jewelry.

Barbara Belmont cut a cool figure behind a microphone, better even than Henry. There were no dessert stragglers. Everybody had finished. Saying that was a tactic. It got everyone thinking she liked them and was on their side.

She waited another minute. Waiters in white shirts and black bow ties scurried around clearing plates. The room gradually quieted until every eye fell on Barbara.

"I'll be brief. As you know, my husband wasn't born in Arizona, but never doubt that he loves it, understands it, and wants it to be better. I often think of how we've grown from a rugged frontier territory into the special place we've become and the major role played by the five Cs."

She paused to gauge the crowd's reaction.

"I can see by your faces you've never heard of the five Cs. Well, tonight I'm going to give you an important history lesson. The five Cs are copper, cotton, cattle, citrus, climate, the industries that built this state. And after November, we'll be adding one more to that list. Can you all guess what it is?"

Someone in the crowd called out, "Vin the Chin!" and that sparked scattered applause.

"That's right, madam, the sixth C—Vin the Chin!"

As the applause grew and became general, Barbara leaned into the microphone and turned her head, pointing back to the restaurant door. "Please welcome the next senator from the great state of Arizona, Mr. Henry Vincent Belmont."

They gave each other Hollywood hugs behind the podium.

"I can't believe you came up with the five Cs all by yourself."

"I'm smart, Henry. Everybody knows that but you."

"Are you plastered already?"

"About to be. Try not to screw this up."

Disengaging, clapping, Henry pointed to Barbara as she exited. "Isn't she something?"

Barbara ducked into the bar. Loud and packed, elbow to elbow. She ordered a shot of bourbon and threw it down. She signaled for another and put that away, too. The booze dulled the disgust she felt.

She signaled for a third drink. She carried it down to the bend in the bar, pulled out her burner, and called Mary. It was a check-in call.

"It's tomorrow. Is everything all right?"

"Yes."

"Is everything a go?"

"Yes."

Too many people were crowded around to say much more, and it was hard to hear.

Barbara asked where she was. Mary lied and said at the office. That was the answer Barbara needed. She threw down the shot and drove to Mary's house.

No lights shone in the little house on South Fourth Street. Only the intermittent blinking of the big TV in the living room broke the darkness. Barbara peered in through the front window and saw Dorothy on the couch, head back against the cushions, sound asleep.

She tried the front door. Locked. She went around to the back. The screen door opened. She stepped inside the Arizona room, used a credit card on the kitchen door, and tiptoed through the living room, shooting Dorothy with her fingers as she walked past.

In Mary's bedroom, she pulled the dresser away from the wall and opened the safe. Empty, all the money gone. At first, Barbara was shocked. Then she thought about it and nodded to herself and was calm again.

I know what happened. I know exactly what happened.

She closed the safe door, wiped it down, and walked past Dorothy again and out the back door. She picked up the takeout from Taco Bandito and went home.

CHAPTER TWENTY-SEVEN

She was drinking a glass of wine when Henry returned from his speech. He complained about the food being cold. Barbara didn't argue. She was the good wife tonight. She microwaved it and they ate on the couch with the television on.

Henry hogged the remote and Barbara let him do it, saying nothing.

Afterward, he went outside and floated in the pool with a drink. When he called for another, Barbara brought it to him without complaining.

On the fifth drink he reached out from his raft and took her hand.

"Know what I think about a lot?"

"What's that?"

"The night we met. 'Memba?"

He drunk-talked about the night they met. Barbara recalled every detail of how they met and Henry had everything wrong. She didn't bother correcting him.

He told her he loved her. Barbara held his hand and listened, smiling, thinking this was his last night of life. She wanted badly to tell him that, just to wipe the sappy look off his face.

But it would have to wait until tomorrow.

When Henry stumbled down the hall to the bedroom, Barbara followed and closed the door and went back out to the pool and called Tommy Logan.

"You're in town, right?"

"Hotel. Sort of a dump. I'm out on the balcony."

"Hope you got a nice view at least."

"Palm trees, big old mountains. I don't know, ain't my style. Too much scenery."

Barbara went over the plan as they'd already discussed it.

After getting the room key from the clerk, Barbara, dressed as Marilyn, would hand it off to Mary, and Mary would lead Henry up to the room. Logan, waiting nearby and watching, would follow them and knock.

Henry would think it was the union man. Mary would think it was Barbara. Henry would tell Mary to open the door and she'd do it. Logan would step inside and handle things.

The cops would find Henry and Mary dead and Marilyn gone and figure the three of them had gathered for some wild fun, only Marilyn had different ideas.

Barbara asked Logan if he had an orphan and a suppressor, and Logan assured her he did. After the deed, Logan would clean out Henry's wallet and Mary's purse, wipe down both, and toss them into the dumpster outside.

The police would look there first, and that was what they wanted. A desperate drug addict, a prostitute killer, took the cash and credit cards, ditched everything else, and ran.

Barbara would drive up the road from the Beautiful Day Motel to a remote spot on the canal. She described for Logan the exact location. Turn east off Fifty-First Avenue down the narrow driveway between two abandoned warehouses.

In back there's nothing but a dark lot. Barbara would be there. While waiting for Tommy, she'd change out of her Marilyn clothes into her original outfit and redo her makeup.

When Tommy showed up, she'd hand him his second payment. She'd promised to give him $10,000 tonight and another $10,000 after Henry and Mary were dead.

Barbara said those words to the Screwdriver with absolute conviction. They were lies. She wasn't going to pay him a nickel. She planned to kill him and dump his body in the canal.

With their transaction complete, Barbara would drive back to the fundraiser, toast the right people, smile, chat, and lie about how wonderful everyone looked for as long as anyone wanted, so there'd be no question she'd been there.

After running through the plan, Barbara threw Logan a curveball. "Something's come up, a teensy-weensy problem."

"I don't like the sound of that."

"Your money isn't where it's supposed to be."

"What do you mean, 'where it's supposed to be'? Where the hell's that?"

"Mary's safe. She emptied it out. I broke into her house earlier tonight and it's gone."

"Wait, you were gonna pay me with money you had to boost? The night before all this, you break into her house to steal my money?"

"There was never a question about getting in. The back door takes MasterCard and she told me the safe's combination."

"I don't care how you got in. All I care about is my money. Ten grand tonight, ten after. That was our agreement."

"I can fix this."

"Deal's off. I came all the way out here for a burger and fries."

"No, no, we're still good."

"No way. Why would she move the money if she didn't know something was up? Use your head, she's onto you."

Barbara walked to the far side of the pool, away from the house in case Henry was up and roaming. The mountain loomed at her shoulder, dark and silent.

"No, she's not. She doesn't suspect anything. I'm her hero. Mary loves me all the way, I'm telling you."

"Jesus, what a waste of time."

"Hear me out, Tommy. Just let me explain."

A strong wind blew through the backyard, swirling and snapping the flaps of the umbrella on the cool deck.

"It's her stepmom. Mary's been worried about her stepmom. That she figured out the combination. See what I'm telling you? She's hiding the money from her, not me."

"Now I'm curious, Doll. How much we talking about? How much was in that safe?"

"Your cut was twenty grand."

"That's not what I asked. How much was in there, total? Like, all of it?"

Barbara hesitated. She was stuck. She paced around the cool deck with the phone to her ear. "You're pushing me, Tommy. I don't like it."

"How much or I'm out."

She paused a long time. "Okay, sure. Thirty grand."

"That's a very nice number. I like it. I want it all, every dollar."

"That wasn't the deal. The deal was twenty grand. Ten and ten."

"Oh, you can change the deal but I can't? Thirty or I walk. Fifteen, fifteen."

"So I get none of Mary's money? I'm shut out? That's my money!" Barbara was shouting. She caught herself and lowered her voice, the words crawling out in an animal growl now. "That money is my money. It belongs to Henry and me. He's *my* husband."

"Can the routine, Doll. You hate his guts."

"What does that have to do with it? He's mine and so is his money. I'm not giving up either one to you, to some chippy or anybody else."

"Don't be greedy. You get Belmont Construction, total control. With Henry gone, it's all yours. You'll make it back ten times, a hundred times. You'll be a rich bitch. You figured out the bitch part a long time ago. Now all you need's the dough."

The kitchen door slid open and Henry stumbled out wearing only white boxers. He stood for a moment looking around, glassy-eyed, trying to figure out where he was. Slowly, he stepped to the edge of the pool and stared into the placid water, wavering on unsteady legs.

"Hang on, Tommy." Barbara held the phone against her chest. "Henry, what the hell?"

He didn't hear or see her. He reached under his boxers and pissed two-handed into the pool as he sang in a voice that rumbled all the way up from the tips of his toes: "*Froggy had a bellyache, oh so bad / Couldn't find his doggie and oh so sad.*"

He shook it a few times, put it back, and walked stiff-legged into the house, still singing.

"Doll? You there? What's going on?"

"Henry's practicing his victory speech. Go ahead."

"You need to look at things from my side. I'm takin' two birthdays. They put the cuffs on me over this, it's life without."

"You're stealing from me, Tommy, and it ticks me the hell fucking off all fucking day. Do you know how much I hate you?"

"Can I take that as a yes?"

Barbara blew a loud sigh. She kicked over one of the deck chairs.

"Doll? You tearing shit up over there? Having a fit for yourself?"

"Yeah, yeah, yeah, I'm having a fit. Okay, you win. Thirty. And fuck you, by the way."

"Like old times."

"Now, listen to me, there's something else."

"Let me guess. You got no idea where she put the money."

"We can find out easy. Tomorrow night, instead of taking off for the canal, I'll go up to the room with you and stick a gun in Mary's cute little ear and ask her. I've found that works good for getting information."

Barbara had wanted no part of the room. That was what she was paying Logan for. The office was one thing, a necessity to get Henry and Mary into the room together. But that was as far as she wanted to go, until Mary's money disappeared.

"What about my first installment? I was supposed to get it tonight."

I scraped together some cash of my own. From the business. Four thou. It's the best I can do.

"That's a shit pile short of fifteen, Doll."

"I told you, I'm tight right now. You'll get all of it. Just later."

"I'm supposed to trust you? After Boston?"

"I don't like this either. I expected that money to be there, but the safe was empty on account of her stepmother. Look, I've got the four with me right now. What hotel are you at? I'll come over."

Logan harrumphed. "No chance."

"You won't tell me where you're staying?"

"I don't like people knowing my locale, if you will. Being hard to find's the opposite of the joint."

"I'm trying to do business with you, Tommy."

"Know what else I don't like? Can't find a Dunkin' Donuts around here."

"Honest to God, you're the worst. Now I know why they let you out early."

"Prison ministry. It pays to believe." He laughed.

"All right, let's do it this way. That spot on the canal, I'll put the four in a bag and leave it there for you. There's a big drainage pipe running into the canal. You can't miss it. I'll leave the bag under the pipe."

"Yeah, that works." From his perch on the balcony, Tommy looked out at the sprawling city. "It don't seem like there'd be much trouble around here. Guys pulling jobs and shit. Place with so many swimming pools. But there's jerks everywhere, I suppose. When will the four be there?"

"I'll leave now. You can pick it up anytime overnight."

"What's to keep me from grabbing the money and running?"

"Not a thing. You could be back in Boston in a few hours. That'd be four grand for a plane ride and a Happy Meal and you'd never hear from me again. But you'd be saying good-bye to twenty-six grand."

"It was a Quarter Pounder."

"Does that tell you how much I want this job done?"

Tommy Logan punched off on the call and turned around. Mary Rose Cleary was sitting in the chair behind him.

"Did you hear your girlfriend? Huh? Yeah, you heard her. My price just went up. I'll need seventeen five tonight and the rest after. If you can't handle the weight, tell me right now."

CHAPTER TWENTY-EIGHT

Cool and confident, legs crossed, Mary had on tight jeans and a sleeveless, low-cut black chiffon blouse. She sat slouched in the chair, hair hanging against her chest. Rings gleamed on the fingers of both hands.

"Are you sticking me up, Mr. Logan? I don't think I like that."

"You see a gun? I got no gun. Nah, I'm taking bids, that's all. I'm a businessman selling my services. American dream. Yeah."

"I should have expected this. All right. You'll get your money."

"Outstanding."

"Now, if we could, let's talk details."

They talked details. The killings of Henry and Barbara Belmont would look like a robbery attempt that tipped over and became a double homicide. The room would be torn up, Barbara's jewelry gone, Henry's money gone.

The cops would wonder why Barbara, dressed like Marilyn Monroe, was dead in a motel room with her husband. Husbands and wives don't go to crappy motels together.

The answer would be drugs, specifically, meth.

Logan would sprinkle some hot ice on the floor to stand up the angle.

Back in Boston, Mickey D'Angelo had made millions dealing crystal and would've made a lot more if not for Dirty Dolly. She was his biggest customer. She treated crystal like candy on Halloween night.

Maybe she was using again and not paying her dealer. Maybe she was selling. Maybe she and Henry had a freaky tryst set up with some hot-rolling mystery guest who couldn't stand the noise of her own blinking anymore and started shooting.

With so much of it pouring across the Mexican border and up to Phoenix for distribution around the country, there'd be a million maybes. The police could spend the rest of their lives following the crystal trail and it would lead nowhere.

Logan leaned his back against the balcony railing. "When the time comes, I got some advice for you, girlie. About the cops."

"Go ahead."

"When they talk to you about this, don't say too much about Dolly. Breadcrumbs, that's all. Let them find out about her past on their own. Makes 'em feel smart. Cops wanna go home at five o'clock. Give 'em a good set of facts to clear the case, and off they go to the wife and kids."

"It's comforting to be in business with a man of such expertise, Mr. Logan."

"What's Doll carrying these days?"

"Colt King Cobra, .357. It's an orphan. She carries it everywhere."

"Thing could take down a hippo. Got a piece of your own?"

"Glock .45. And yes, I'm more than proficient."

"Bring it and hope you don't have to use it. But if this shit bucket blows up, I want you to be ready."

They talked for thirty minutes. Logan went through the plan again step by step, then, saying he was curious, asked Mary about her life.

She told a fantastic story of her travels, her adventures and accomplishments at college and after. She talked about the rich men she'd dated across Europe, her love of art, and the book she'd written about Cézanne, his late style.

Every word fiction. It was the life she'd dreamed about as a girl and knew now, finally, that she'd never have.

Staring, Logan listened carefully, waiting until she'd finished to speak. "I gotta ask, you sure you wanna go through with this? This world you're walking into, it ain't your world."

"Yet here I am."

"Thing I know for sure, no bullshit, is Dirty Dolly Hatcher don't go down easy. She's like a roach. She'll find a corner."

"Yes, I've discovered she's—adaptable."

Logan stared some more, eyes hard, intense.

"Something's troubling you, Mr. Logan."

"Girl like you doing a job like this, I don't get it."

"You don't trust me, Mr. Logan?"

"Everything you got going on and you want two people dead? That's all I'm saying. It's nothing to me. Doll's been on my list a long time. But I don't get why you're doing this."

"You don't have to get it."

"Put it this way, I'm asking and you need to tell me."

"Don't push me, Mr. Logan. My business is my business."

"Tonight we're in the same business. I want an answer."

"Henry Belmont betrayed me. So did Barbara. Does that satisfy you?"

"That's always been enough for me, but you?"

"I was afraid of this, that when the time came, you'd lose your courage."

"Be careful with your words there. Talking that way ain't conducive to what you call human longevity."

Mary tsk-tsked. "I was afraid you'd piss yourself and I'd have to wish you good night."

Logan's face turned red. The muscles in his jaw rippled as he stared. Then, slowly, his temper cooled, an admiring smile crossed his lips, and he nodded. And Mary, as she'd done the whole time they were talking, only looked at him sideways, never straight in the eye.

She thought him grotesque and insignificant. He thought her doable.

"Have I upset you, Mr. Logan?"

"You'll hand over the first seventeen five tonight?"

"Give me an hour."

He nodded and stared some more. "Maybe after this we could, ah, you know, have a little get-together."

Bored, without looking at him: "I'll be sure to comb my hair."

"I could start liking this town." He turned around and leaned on the railing and looked out at the long valley of blinking lights and screaming sirens. "Wonder if I could be one of them Sunbelt guys, wearing plaid pants and golfing alla time?"

CHAPTER TWENTY-NINE

It rained Thursday afternoon, a violent roof-pounding monsoon. But the dry ground had sucked it up and made it disappear as fast as it had fallen. The night breeze blew pastry clouds past a curving desert moon.

The Beautiful Day Motel had a green metal roof, a white cinder-block exterior, green doors, and reasonable rates. The buzzing neon sign said so, only two burned-out letters.

The parking lot fronted Fifty-First Avenue. The office anchored the far south end of the building. Mary drove into the lot in Dorothy's Prius, turned past the office, drove along the row of numbered doors, and parked.

Henry had followed her the whole way and rolled up beside her.

It was a slow night. At least three-quarters of the spaces were empty.

But three men sat on traffic blocks just down from their cars. One had bare feet and no shirt. They shared a bottle. They eyed Henry's car closely.

Mary killed the engine, got out, and walked around to Henry's door. He fingered the driver's window down. "This is a major dumpola. Couldn't you at least have lined up a Holiday Inn?"

"Cheer up, Henry. It could be worse."

"How?"

She gave a nervous laugh. Her heart thundered like runaway horses. How could he not hear that? *I can barely hear myself talk.* "I'll have to think about that."

"What're you wearing, anyway? I've never seen that before."

"They call it a shirtdress. Kate Spade." She straightened, bent her hips, and put her palms flat against her thighs. "Do you like it? It's versatile. You can wear it with heels or sneakers. I went shopping for clothes."

Don't talk so much, don't explain. Stay calm.

"I don't understand why you're wearing it now. The other day you showed up at work wearing another dress I'd never seen."

"That was a cocktail dress."

"Nobody was having a cocktail party."

"That's true, Henry, but it's kind of literal. You can wear a cocktail dress without having cocktails. Actually, if you must know, I was going out later."

"Where? I didn't know anything about that."

"Places. You don't have to know everything I do."

"I know you can wear a cocktail dress without having cocktails. But you'd never worn it before. And now I find out you're going places with the election coming up and you've got this fancy dress and I've never seen that before either."

"It's not that fancy. Let's call it utilitarian."

"That's all I'm saying. Something's going on with you."

"There are lots of things about me you don't know, Henry. Maybe when I'm not working, I'm a different person."

"Different how?"

"Maybe I do exciting things and have exciting thoughts."

"Yeah, like what? This I got to hear."

Mary, what are you doing? This isn't the time to assert yourself. It's too late for that. Stop, stop. She felt pounding in her ears. She needed to come up with something fast.

"I read a lot."

"That's what I figured. Your exciting thing is books?"

Bring it back, Mary. Say whatever you have to say to bring it back.

"The most exciting thing I do is work for you, Henry. Every day, just being around you."

He waved an end to the conversation as though he were trying to get rid of a pesky fly.

"Okey-dokey. How about I just go down to the office and get the key."

She walked down the sidewalk. Sitting behind the wheel, Henry watched her go. Her legs and bottom looked nice in that dress. Kate Spade. Why would she wear a designer dress to meet a union guy in a sleazy motel? And what was she wearing a cocktail dress for?

If she's getting too hifalutin, too confident, that could be a problem.

Fifty grand. That's no problem at all.

Froggy had a bellyache, oh so bad...

At the office, Mary skipped around the corner to the parking lot behind the building. Barbara's red Ford SUV was there. Mary hurried into the passenger seat and closed the door.

"I think he knows. He's asking questions about my clothes. He never once asked me questions like that."

"I guarantee he's thinking about money, nothing else. Stay steady. Don't flip out now."

"I'm not flipping out. Why would you choose a drug motel?"

"Ambience. Kind of fits the job at hand, don't you think?"

"I'm serious. There's too many eyes."

"They're addicts. Whatever they see tonight, they won't remember tomorrow, and nothing they say would be worth anything in court anyway. They might as well be trees. This place is perfect."

"I guess you're right."

"How do I look?"

"Lovely. Marilyn herself never looked so lovely."

Barbara wore round glasses and white gloves. The lush blond wig sat high on her head, all butter curls and tumbling waterfalls.

She had on stiletto heels, hoop earrings, and a low-cut red blouse showing a canyon of cleavage. She figured that's where the clerk's eyes would go.

Her eyebrows were dark streaks, her lips a glossy plum. The Macy's counter clerk had described the lipstick as a color sensation, the perfect choice for any occasion.

Especially a murder, Barbara thought.

"All right, Marilyn's off. This is it. Are you ready?"

"I don't understand Henry asking me about my dress. That threw me."

"Don't get hung up on that. It's nothing. I asked you a question. Are you ready?"

"I think so."

"We're done thinking. The plan is set. Now all we have to do is carry it out."

"I'm ready."

"You better be, because what happens tonight, right now, is the rest of our lives. There's no mistakes tonight, okay?"

"Absolutely." Mary breathed and let it out slowly. "Let's do this."

"Stay put. I'll be right back."

Barbara went around to the office. The bell over the door chimed. The first thing she noticed was the wall camera behind the desk hanging loose on its strut, the lens pointing uselessly at the floor. Barbara smiled to herself. She'd always been lucky at crime, and her good fortune was showing itself again.

The clerk had to be seventy-five. He was tall, sweaty, colorless, dull-eyed. His voice was a toneless drone, barely human, as if the sound of the bell had activated it.

"Welcome to a Beautiful Day. How can we make your day more beautiful?"

He never looked up. Normally, that would've bothered Barbara, but not tonight. She paid cash and showed a phony driver's license. The clerk wrinkled his face as he read it.

His lips didn't move when he spoke. "Mindy Turk Samuels of Bentonville, Arkansas. Five foot six, one hundred and twenty pounds."

Barbara, the former high school beauty queen, struggled to suppress a laugh. Turn-ons include sunsets, walks on the beach, powerful handguns, and simple carbohydrates.

He took her cash, banged on the keyboard with two fingers, and handed the license back with the key. "Have a beautiful evening at a Beautiful Day."

Barbara went back to the SUV and got in. "Cadaver behind the counter and no camera. Couldn't have worked out better. You're up, Mary."

"I can't believe this is it."

"This is it."

They gripped each other's hands over the console, a final, silent show of unity. Mary hopped out of the car and returned to Henry Belmont.

"That took forever."

"Some old guy in there."

"They like me, the old folks. The dinks. Double income, no kids. My numbers guru says they're solid behind me."

"You're on your way for sure, Henry." She was talking to him through his car window. "Let's go. We'll wait up in the room."

"Upstairs? My football knee's killing me. You couldn't get anything on the first floor?"

Barbara had been definite, second floor only. No cars, fewer people walking past.

"You can do it, Henry. It's fourth and goal on the two. Let's push the ball into that end-zone area."

"You don't know the first thing about football."

"And I take great pride in that. It's not a good idea to sit out here. Somebody might recognize you."

"Where is this union guy, anyway?"

Mary pretended to look around the parking lot. "Not here yet, I guess. Gee. I'm sure he'll be along in a minute."

"Does he have a name? You never told me his name."

She froze. With all the planning she'd done, all the possibilities she'd played out in her mind, coming up with a name hadn't been one of them.

Come on, Mary, any name will do. Out of millions of possibilities, she couldn't come up with a single one. Her mouth had gone dry.

Henry saved her. "Ah, it doesn't matter. Why would it matter? If he's got the money, what difference does it make?"

"You're right. What difference does it make?"

"Let's get this over with."

"Come on, I'll help you up the stairs. Number eleven, second floor."

Henry stepped out of his car and the two of them started up the stairs. But for the rumble of traffic out on Fifty-First Avenue, the night was soundless.

CHAPTER THIRTY

Behind the motel, Tommy Logan knuckled on the driver's window and motioned for Barbara to get out. He wore work boots, a wrinkled blue ball cap, jeans, and a tattered gray sweatshirt, loose fitting and untucked.

She spoke out the window. "Give them a minute to get up there."

"They're there by now. Come on, it's time."

"You get the four thou okay?"

"You think I'd be here if I didn't? Let's go."

She got out of the car. Logan stepped back to give her Marilyn getup the once-over. "I gotta say, Doll." He nodded as if impressed. "You look cheap."

"Thank you."

"You're welcome."

Together they headed down the sidewalk, careful to make sure the clerk had returned to his back-room quarters before passing in front of the glass. Barbara led the way up the stairs. Sniffing at her heels, Logan pulled gloves out of his pocket and put them on. He held a gun down against his leg.

At number eleven, Barbara knuckled on the door. The latch came undone, Mary opened it, and Barbara stepped inside.

The room looked like they all do. Two double beds, a bureau with a TV on top, paintings of flowers on popcorn walls. The air conditioner was busted. The powerful smell of sweat hung in the air, and the heat was choking.

Mary was sitting on the first bed and Henry the second. He studied the dolled-up blonde with the plum lips. It took a moment to register. "Barbara? What the hell are you doing here?" Confusion rearranged his face. "This isn't what it looks like, Barb."

"Shut up, Henry. Everything with you is exactly what it looks like."

"Yeah, shut up, Henry." Logan walked in and ankled the door closed behind him.

"Who the hell are you?"

Logan marched over and pressed the barrel of his gun against Henry's forehead. "This is who I am. Any more questions, friend?"

Henry's eyes bulged out of his head and his hands flew up. "All right, all right, I get it. That's who you are. Pleased to meet you, sir."

"That's my man right there." Standing just inside the door, Barbara spat contempt from the corner of her mouth. "Get on with it, Tommy. Let's find out what she did with the money. I gotta get back."

Feeling the first stings of panic, Mary gave Barbara a wide-eyed look. Whatever was happening, she didn't like it.

"This is my play, Doll." Logan grabbed Barbara by the arm, dragged her deeper into the room, and threw her onto the bed beside Henry, peeling her purse off her shoulder as he did.

"Ow! You're yanking my arm off! What the hell!"

As soon as Barbara hit the mattress, Logan drew his arm back and gave her a sweeping backhanded slap. Her face snapped to one side, leaving her Marilyn wig off-kilter over one ear.

"Did you really think I'd let it go, Doll?"

"Tommy! Jesus, that frickin' hurt!"

"Thirteen years."

He whacked her again, going back the other way, and the wig went haywire over that ear. She wiped blood from her lip with the back of her hand.

"I shoulda known. God, I shoulda known. You're such a weasel, Tommy."

"You got a mouth and I got a gun. Guess who wins that one every time." Logan laughed, showing all his crooked teeth.

He opened Barbara's purse, found the Colt Cobra .357, and held it up. "What's this here, Doll? You come to my party strapped? You don't trust me, eh? That hurts my feelings." Logan snorted. "Hope it ain't traceable."

Mary piped up. "It's not. It's the orphan, the one I told you about."

"Smart." Tommy put the Colt in his pocket and tossed the purse on the bed. "Rule number one, never carry a piece with parents."

Barbara's angry eyes leapt to Mary. "You're working with this one? Is that what this is?" Her face bloomed red and she launched off the bed toward Mary.

She didn't get far. Logan put her down with a knee to the stomach. Barbara curled up on the floor, choking and coughing. Logan ordered Henry to get her back on the bed, after which Barbara continued glaring at Mary.

"You played me. You're working with the Screwdriver. I must be losing my edge. Swear to God. How did I not see this coming? Congratulations." Barbara held her hands out and clapped as if it took a lot of effort.

"Number two in your class but number one on the street. I'm impressed. I was supposed to be the one schooling you. Turns out the opposite. Do you know what this means? You're the queen bitch now, the baddest bitch in the desert. I'm being serious here. You aced your SATs tonight, sugar."

Logan stepped toward Henry, waving his gun. "That talking hurts my ears bad. Shut her up or I'll kill you right now."

Henry clamped his palm over Barbara's mouth. She kept trying to talk and he made the vise tighter. She bit him and Henry hollered and they wrestled on the bed until he got her under control and she quieted.

There was a knock at the door and a barely audible male voice outside.

"Maid service."

"Open up." Logan nodded at Mary.

She hesitated. Somebody's at the door? Nobody else is supposed to be here. This isn't going the way we planned. Maybe Logan was right. Maybe this isn't my world.

Logan nodded again with more urgency. Mary got the message and opened the door. Jimmy No Lips elbowed Mary aside and walked past her. "I need something clear up front. I don't do windows."

He wore sneakers, black sweatpants, and an ill-fitting open-necked pullover jersey. Some kind of large tattoo colored most of his neck. A shiny gold cross dangled from his left ear. His face broke open with a sloppy grin.

"How you people doin' this evenin'?"

Barbara, from the bed: "That settles it. This ain't a Mensa meeting."

Mary spun on Logan. "Just you, nobody else. That was the deal, Mr. Logan. Who is this man?"

"My aide-de-camp." Logan waved his gun at Jimmy. "By the look of that cute dress she got on, I'd say that little girl's carrying. Check the left pocket, you wouldn't mind."

Mary jumped back at Jimmy's approach. "Wait. What're you doing? Don't touch me, you creep. What is this?"

She tried to reach into the pocket, but Jimmy got hold of her arm and stopped her. He fished the Glock out with Mary fighting to get it back, all the while barking at Tommy.

"You told me to bring it, Logan!"

"I did at that." Tommy shook his head as if saddened. "You did what I told you. And you're supposed to be the brainy one. You just set yourself up for a nifty double-murder rap, girlie."

Jimmy was wrestling with Mary. "She's a pisser, Tommy. Smells good, too." He was standing behind her, his arm wrapped around her middle. He held her so tight her feet came off the floor. She kicked like a bug.

Tommy took the Glock from Jimmy and slipped his own gun into his pocket, leaving him holding only the Glock. "Thing is, girlie, if you're gonna bring a piece to a job, you gotta be quick, like a gunslinger. Ain't that right, Jimmy?"

"Calamity Jane or one of them, you betcha."

Mary kept fighting and kicking. "I trusted you, Logan."

"No shit. That was a definite wrongo."

Jimmy hooted as he struggled to hang on to Mary. "I'm likin' this one, Tommy. She's dumbass fine."

"All right, now, I want to call a meeting about a crucial subject." Tommy Logan had the stage and liked it. He paused for effect. He folded his arms on his chest and scratched his cheek with the barrel of the Glock. "Subject wise, it has to do with the money from this one's safe."

He pointed the gun at Mary.

"I need to know where you stashed the thirty Gs. Or was it thirty-five?" He wrinkled his face as if in deep contemplation. He made a clicking sound in his mouth. "See, I'm getting different stories, and when it comes to money, I don't like different stories. It makes me, what do you call it, disturbed. So let's hear it."

Mary reached back and tried to gouge Jimmy's eyes. He cackled as he bent his head from side to side to escape her reach.

Barbara, in a taunting voice: "Got news for you, Tommy. There wasn't thirty Gs in that safe. No, it's more like a hundred ten." Looking straight at Mary: "A hundred ten grand stolen from my husband."

Henry startled. "Mary?"

"I had a feeling this trip would pay off handsome." Logan stepped over to Mary, pressing his face against hers. "The hundred ten, where's it at?"

Mary kicked and spat.

"Easy or hard, up to you."

She wouldn't stop fussing. Logan belted her. Her eyes rolled up. Drool hung from her lips. He belted her again, harder, then again, and she gave up.

"In the trunk of my car! ... Outside! ... Take it and let me go!"

Logan whacked her one more time. "If you're lying to me, I'll break you, unnastand?" He pulled a suppressor from his pocket and screwed it into the barrel of the Glock. He pulled back the slide and racked a round into the pipe.

Panicked, Henry Belmont practically came off the bed.

"No! Don't do this! I can get you a lot more than a hundred ten thousand, Logan. I know some very rich people. I can get money here, tonight. Lots of money. Logan. One phone call."

Barbara sighed. "Don't make it worse, Henry. Do what you need to do, Tommy, and when you're done, go straight to hell."

In white-faced shock, Henry Belmont turned his attention to Mary.

"I brought you on. I gave you everything." He exploded in rage. "I trusted you! You betrayed me! Everything I've done for you! I brought you out here to help me!"

"I'm sorry, Mr. Belmont." Her voice came from behind the moon. "This isn't a good day."

Henry swiveled his eyes to Tommy. "Go ahead and shoot! You don't have what it takes! You're a damn coward! You don't have the guts!"

Tommy Logan shot Henry Belmont between the eyes. The muffled explosion sounded like someone using a broom to beat a rug. His body dropped across Barbara's lap.

As she looked down at her dead husband, her mouth twitched.

A terrible silence fell over the stinking room.

Logan nodded at Jimmy. "Escort our girlie here outside. When you get eyes on the money, call me, and go to the place by the canal, like we talked. Wait there for me."

"Ain't you gonna do her, Tommy?"

"I'll be down." Logan turned to Barbara with hell in his heart. "Thirteen years. I'm gonna take my time."

Jimmy dragged Mary out the door.

CHAPTER THIRTY-ONE

Mary stumbled down the motel steps, clutching at the railing, Jimmy behind her with a fistful of her hair. When they got to the back of the Prius, he grabbed her by the shoulders and spun her around and pressed the length of his body against hers and kissed her.

She fought, trying to shove him away, but his hand still gripped her hair, and he yanked her head back to do it again. This time Mary relaxed and put her arms around him. "Not in the parking lot."

"I knew it the minute I seen you. You got sex in your eyes."

They were openmouthed and grinding against the car, Mary tugging at Jimmy's shirt. "Let's find a place. Let's go to the canal like Tommy said."

"Yeah, yeah, yeah."

"It's been a slow night for me, you know. So far. I need some."

Jimmy squeak-laughed. "You're a real slice, lady."

"I am so friggin' ready. Oh, my God. Do that, do that."

"Like this?"

"Oh, oh. Jimmy, let me just do this. Oh." Mary tried to shove her hand down between them. But with the pressure of Jimmy's body against hers, she couldn't force it through. "Not here, no, no, Jimmy. Not here. The canal."

He was strong for a rack of bones. She couldn't get him off her to push her hand down.

"Jimmy, Jimmy, Jimmy. Look. Jimmy, look over here."

Next to them, fifteen feet away, a shirtless man lay unconscious on the ground, using a traffic block for a pillow.

"I don't want to give him a show. Not for free, baby. No way, Jimmy."

"He's dead. Look at him. He's a goner. He's in the ozone layer."

"He's not dead, Jimmy. He needs to pay to see what we're gonna do." She reached her hand between them again, but Jimmy held her tight. "Let's go to the canal, baby. Come on, let's get out of here and go to the canal."

"All right, all right." He loosened his grip and stepped back. "But money first. I wanna see the money. Open the trunk."

"Screw the money. Come on, Jimmy."

"Tommy's orders. Do what I tell you. Open it."

She got the keys from her pocket and opened the hatch. Jimmy stuck his head inside and saw the plastic drop cloths. "What's this shit?"

"My house needs a paint job. Look in the sack underneath."

When he reached in deeper, Mary lifted her skirt and pulled the .380 from her thigh holster and stuck it against his neck.

"I'll use it, Jimmy boy. Better believe I will."

"Nice move. But you ain't got the balls, not in public."

He tried to straighten up. Mary slammed the hatch down on his head with a loud *thunk*. Jimmy crumpled, half in the trunk and half out. She grabbed his ear and practically twisted it off to get him standing again.

She found his gun under his shirt and tossed it into the trunk and slammed the lid. She stuck her gun in his back and walked him to the driver's door, shoved him behind the wheel, and hustled around to the passenger seat.

"Call Tommy. Say, 'The money's here.' That's all I want to hear. One extra word and I'll blow a hole in you."

Jimmy got his cell phone out of his pocket. He juggled it and moaned as he tried to focus on the screen. He did what he was told, said only those three words.

Mary heard Tommy respond, "Take her to the canal. I won't be long."

Jimmy clicked off on the call. Mary leaned over, stuck the key in the ignition, turned the engine over, and ordered Jimmy to drive.

"I'm seeing things here. I don't think I can be, like, a responsible driver right now."

"Do it."

She pressed the .380 against his jaw for encouragement. Jimmy pulled the Prius across the parking lot and onto Fifty-First Avenue. He drove north. Mary got her tequila bottle out of the glove and took a long swig.

"You guys were planning to kill me. Set me up for Henry and Barbara."

"Shit. No way. You're dreaming."

"Cops find me dead at the canal by my own gun and figure I did them at the motel first and came here."

"That's not it. That's Tommy, he talks a lot. That's just Tommy sayin' stuff, over and over, like a recording. He don't quit."

"Let's go, step on it."

They passed a Circle K, Food City, Comfort Inn, AutoZone, trashy apartment complexes. Traffic whipped along. Burned-out streetlights, empty sidewalks. They could see warehouses and industrial buildings coming up. They were set back off the road on both sides.

"It's always this and that with Tommy. He's big with words, but he don't mean what he says. You get what I'm saying?"

"He put a bullet in Henry's head."

"Yeah, but come on, that guy. I mean, who cares? He's nobody."

"Where's my money?"

"What money? It's in the trunk."

"The money I gave Tommy. I want it back."

"Man, my friggin' head. You really hurt me. I can't remember shit."

"Last night I gave Logan seventeen and a half grand. That's my money, Jimmy. You guys picked up another four grand at the canal. Remember?"

"Oh, yeah. Well, he wears this thing, Tommy. A cash thing, like, around his belly. It's like a—I don't what it is. Keeps his money in there."

"A money belt?"

"Whatever. It's in there, all of it."

"The four grand will be my tip from Barbara for my evening's work. The canal. Come on, come on. Drive."

Jimmy blinked to clear his eyes and pointed over the steering wheel. "It's up ahead a ways. If I can see. You messed me up, girl. I got people, like, breaking dishes in my head."

He went another two blocks and turned right into a driveway between two abandoned warehouses. A *No Trespassing* sign spray-painted with graffiti hung on a half-fallen chain-link fence. The chain that was supposed to block access was down, and they bumped over it.

Jimmy inched the Prius around behind the buildings. Nothing back there. No lights, no cars, no people, only litter. The parking lot backed up to a line of trees and brush along the canal.

He pulled in under the trees and killed the engine. They got out and Mary ordered Jimmy to sit on the ground with his back against the front of the car.

"I'll get all dirty."

"Sit."

He obeyed. "This ain't what I had in mind, you know what I'm saying, between you and me. What would be happening. I thought we was, like, on."

"Dear God."

"I smell water. I bet there's water down in the canal. Water's the best. Let's sail away, you and me. I know how to sail real good from home. We'll take a voyage. My steady boy said ship ahoy." He laughed crazily.

"Why don't you shut up, Jimmy."

"I thought me and you was gonna have some fun."

"You must be joking."

"What's the plan, what're you gonna do?"

"Wait for your friend."

"Here? In the bushes like a couple mangy dogs?"

"Shut up. Swear to God, Jimmy. Don't make me."

"Make you what?" His mood flipped and he became belligerent. "You gonna handle two of us when Tommy comes, eh, girlie? You think Tommy's gonna just hand over that cash? Seventeen Gs? No, twenty-one Gs. You don't know Tommy Logan. Might be it'll turn out with you down there."

He threw his chin toward the canal. "In the morning when the sun comes up everybody'll look down and see this girl in a nice dress floating down there in the water. 'What happened there? Oh, my goodness. Did she go for a dip? Maybe she's having a little rest for herself.'"

"I won't say it again."

"When they find your friend, that'll make it two dead ladies in one night." He laughed, bravely at first. Then his throat shut down and squeezed the sound, and his confidence vanished and fear gripped his face.

"I don't even like him. Everybody thinks Tommy and me are tight, but we ain't. That's bullshit. We grew up in the same neighborhood. Codman Square, Dorchester. Norfolk Street. But I know plenty of people from all over. Southie, Savin Hill. I got friends, and I look out for them and they look out for me. Screw the Screwdriver. Who the hell's Tommy Logan, anyways?"

Jimmy sat facing the canal with his legs stretched out in front of him and his palms flat in the dirt at his sides. Any move he made to get to Mary would take time, but she kept the gun on him anyway.

She looked over the top of the car toward the driveway.

Tommy should be here any minute. Thinking he's smart, thinking his plan has worked. He'll come in strutting and I'll shut that down quick.

I'm going to enjoy the look on your face, Tommy.

"Can I ask you a question, girlie?"

"Shut up."

Jimmy spat and watched it land in the dirt between his knees. Head lolling, he sat in a posture of defeat, shoulders slumped. His hollow eyes looked like bullet holes in a dumpster.

"That plastic shit in the trunk ain't for paintin', is it?"

Mary kept watch on the driveway. No approaching head-lights, no sign of the Screwdriver. Jimmy No Lips asked the same question again and again and again, louder and more insistent each time, until the fear overtook him and he was shouting.

"What's the plastic shit for, girlie! Tell me! Tell me!"

Mary heard a terrible sound. The bad people were screaming in her head and that awful smell was everywhere, in her nose, in the air over the canal, and all over the smoldering city.

With his voice rising, shaking from panic, Jimmy asked his question again, until Mary Rose Cleary shot him in the mouth. The bullet exploded out the back of his head.

"It's not for painting houses."

She dragged Jimmy's body deeper into the bushes and called Fat Frankie Santiago.

"We're going to be outdoors tonight, Frankie. Along the Grand Canal near the 10. I like it that way. With the moon watching us do it."

She gave him directions and crouched in the brush behind the car to wait.

CHAPTER THIRTY-TWO

The first thing Mary noticed was a change in the sound of the traffic along Fifty-First Avenue. That's him. That's Tommy. But she couldn't be sure.

Maybe the breeze had shifted and distorted the sound.

Then she saw the glimmer of headlights coming down the driveway. The vehicle entered the parking lot and stopped. The engine purred.

Take a good look around, Tommy. Hey, over here.

Thirty long seconds passed.

Come on, Tommy. I'm not going to send up a flare. Let's get it on.

The vehicle began to move again, inching slowly forward.

Now we're in business. Keep coming, Tommy. We're going to see what you've got. How a man faces death says everything about him. Let's see how you die, Tommy.

The vehicle rolled across the parking lot toward the trees and the Prius underneath them. It stopped with its headlights on. The driver's door opened and someone stepped out.

Looking straight into the bright lights, Mary couldn't be sure what she was seeing. A vague figure appeared by the open driver's door, and there was movement. Looking, looking, looking harder, she saw the shadow of a second person standing beside the first.

"Oh, Jimmy! Jimmy lad, where are you?"

The voice belonged to Barbara Belmont.

You're supposed to be dead. The Screwdriver was supposed to kill you.

Mary emerged from the brush holding the .380 with two hands. Barbara recognized her shape in the glow of the headlights.

"Well, look at you. I can't tell you how impressed I am, once again."

"Hello there, Barb. I didn't expect to see you again."

"This is my specialty, isn't it? Men trying to kill me." She made a dismissive sound. "It doesn't ever work out for them, but do they learn?"

Holding the gun steady, Mary stood perfectly still. "Turn off the headlights."

Barbara Belmont reached into the cab and did so. Mary waited for her eyes to adjust and stepped closer. She saw the Ford SUV and Barbara, the blond wig crooked on her head, standing behind Tommy Logan.

She had her right arm curled around his neck, holding him up. In her left hand was a gun pressed to his temple.

Tommy stood awkwardly, bent sideways at the waist. He'd swung his left arm across his body to support his right arm, which hung limp. Blood dripped off his fingers.

Looking over Logan's shoulder, Barbara grinned.

"Remember I told you Henry carried a little Beretta when he got nervous, going to his political meetings." She held the gun out quickly for Mary to see and returned it to Tommy's head. "Had it under his belt. The genius here, Mr. Tommy Logan of Norfolk Street, Dorchester, never checked."

Logan raised his head on a loose neck. "You're a dirty bitch, Doll."

Barbara whacked him on his wounded arm with the Beretta. "Be nice, Tommy."

He open-mouth screamed, fell to one knee, and struggled up again. "Goddammit! Oh, damn, damn! Oh, God!"

"You shot him."

"It was the least I could do, sugar."

"Where's my Glock? And the spent shell from Henry?"

"Don't worry, I ditched the gun and the shell." That was a lie. The gun was in the SUV and Barbara had put the shell in her pocket in case things didn't work out. That was what her gut had told her to do, and her gut was the best GPS she knew.

"I'm supposed to believe you. That gun killed Henry and my prints are all over it."

"Mine, too. I loaded it at the range, remember? Don't worry, nobody'll ever find it." Barbara nodded at Mary's gun. "Where'd you get that mankiller?"

With one hand, and still holding the .380 in place, Mary lifted her skirt and showed the thigh holster and a lot more.

Barbara gave her a wide smile. "You've definitely captured the crown. You're the new queen bitch. I'm proud of you."

"I've earned it."

"What about Jimmy? Where's Jimmy at?"

"Dead." She nodded toward the bushes.

"A banner evening for varmint control. Where does that leave us?"

Mary stepped closer, staring, the skin around her eyes pulled tight, her mouth clenched and small. "Let's start with you putting the Beretta down, Barb."

"I'll keep it if it's all the same." She moved her head farther behind Tommy Logan. She knew it would take a fine shot to nail her. Then again, Mary had skills. But shooting a paper target at the range was a different sport altogether.

"Barb. The gun."

"How about we skip the unpleasant stuff. Haven't we had enough of that for one night? All you're going to do is get us both lugged."

"You brought Logan in to kill me. You betrayed me." Mary pronounced every letter of B-E-T-R-A-Y-E-D, with a long hold on the *A*. "You could've taken my hundred and ten grand and laughed your way home. It's not like I could go to the police over stolen money."

"But I'd still have Henry and he'd still have the company. That required radical surgery."

"You said yourself you wanted him gone and when I came along, you saw your chance. That's all I was to you, a way of getting rid of him."

"Listen to you, all heartbroken. Gunned up and heartbroken."

"I was ready to go all the way with you. Us, together."

"Yet you turned around and hired Logan away to kill me."

"I didn't wreck it, you did. You turned first, Barb. Are you forgetting that?"

"And you jumped on the train after me, so here we are. But you know what, there's another way out of this."

Mary waited, finger on the trigger. The only sounds to occupy the next moments were the moans of a wounded Tommy Logan.

"Way I see it, Red, standing here now, we both got exactly what we want."

"How do you figure?"

"You still got your money and Henry's gone. And I've got Belmont Construction to myself and you can be there with me every step. Running the money end all by yourself."

Mary made an unbelieving face. "Now? After tonight?"

"Absolutely after tonight. Why not? You just have to believe. Act two."

"Never thought of you as an optimist, Barb."

"Love messes with all of us, doesn't it? Twists everything inside out and upside down until you don't know where the ground's at. Let's raise the curtain on act two. Who knows where we go from here?"

Tommy lifted his thousand-pound head. "Don't buy it, girlie. She'll stick you in the back again. That's what she does."

Gritting her teeth, Barbara jammed the gun harder against his temple. He yowled and bent his head practically off his shoulders to get away from it.

"I need a doctor, Doll. I'm bleeding to death here ..." He gave a tortured cry. "From where you fucking shot me!"

She put her mouth close to his ear. "Listen carefully, Tommy. This is important for you to understand. I ... don't ... care."

The breeze kicked up and died, kicked up and died. Gusting, it smelled like the earlier rain that had come in with a roar and tiptoed away like a burglar.

"Look, sugar, we both made a move and it didn't work out. Know what that tells me?"

"What does that tell you, Barb? Fill me in."

"Like I been saying, we're exactly alike, you and me. Grifters born with the wrong equipment, gun honeys turning over rocks thinking we could maybe find something good underneath. Like, I don't know, happiness. Or a man." Barbara laughed bitterly. "Gave up on that one, right? Not on this earth. That leaves money and I'll take it. Every day. Long green. "

"You're stuck in a dream." Mary's voice was cold. "Let's get real."

"You're right, I'm dreaming. Forget I said it. I don't play the romantic too good, do I? So, what, we're going to shoot each other? I'm done with that. Does more shooting make sense to you? It shouldn't, because there's a better way and it's right in front of us."

"I'm listening."

"Say we're even and stick with Plan A."

"Not quite even, Barb. There's something you don't know."

"Yeah, what's that?"

"The Dame-Burma necklace you lied to me about? I've got it."

Barbara felt a jolt of anger ride through her body. "My necklace?" She nodded in reluctant admiration. "You stole my necklace? Bitch, you are good."

"Ricky Peel's necklace. You stole it from him first, probably the same night you killed him. Am I right?"

"I'm gonna need that back."

"Sorry, I earned it."

"Only trouble is, you can't unload it. Every police agency in the world is looking for it. Make so much as a phone call about it and you're done. Why do you think I haven't sold it?"

"I'll figure something out. You must know by now I'm good at that."

"Think through what you're doing. What's your plan, exactly? You gonna shoot me and this hump, too?" She tilted her head toward Logan.

Mary's face hadn't changed. She hadn't moved a muscle. She held the gun high with her arms bracketing her cheeks.

"That means three bodies. You think you can ditch three bodies and walk?" Barbara smacked her lips in doubt. "You might could handle this one and his late associate. A couple out-of-town clowns nobody knows are here anyway. Throw me in, and you're going to ring a lot of bells. I don't see the point."

"Revenge."

Barbara tossed her head and let out a bottom-of-the-belly laugh. "So you're back to that? Your fave. You never told me what you did to your girl at Winchester."

"Her house mysteriously burned to the ground. She got lucky."

"You're something else, sugar. But maybe it's my turn to tell you something you don't know."

"What's that?"

"I have Tony."

"Your cop friend?"

"He knows where I'm at right now, this very moment. Something happens to me, a whole bunch of badges pay you a visit, cuff you up, and it's bye-bye, Mary Rose Cleary. See what I'm saying? Exactly alike."

That wasn't true. Tony had no idea where she was.

"I have to say, I admire you, too, Barb."

"History books call what we have here a fucking impasse."

There was a long quiet. The hot breeze whistled down the canal.

"You don't think I'm being real with you, but I got proof in my pocket."

"Proof that your heart is true, Barb? I'd love to see that."

"You're going to let me show you without shooting me, right?"

Mary didn't answer. She stood perfectly still, arms extended.

"Yeah, you will. You're doing good over there. Nice and calm and you're going to stay that way. Think of something peaceful. Think of whale calls. Nah, whale calls piss me off. Think of a nice musical number. That always does it for me. You ready?"

"Show me, show me. I want to see."

"I'll show you. Now I'm gonna reach into my pocket."

Moving slowly, Barbara tightened her grip around Tommy Logan's neck. She transferred the gun from her left hand to her right. With her left hand free, she reached into her pocket and pulled out two small metal tubes.

"Know what these are? Cohibas. One for you and one for me."

"I made fifty phone calls. Where'd you get them?"

"You don't think I know people? I brought them. For us. To celebrate the end of our common problem."

"You had them with you. Before all this happened."

"That's right. In my pocket. They were for me and you. Like I say, proof."

Mary stepped closer. She began to think she had Barbara all wrong. She saw her split bottom lip and black eye from Logan's blows, and it did something to her. "This creep hit you pretty hard, didn't he? He really messed you up."

Barbara shrugged. "Working the night shift you can run into anything."

"I don't like seeing you that way." Mary's tone had softened, and some of the anger had leaked out of her voice.

"Got my makeup in the car. So are we doing this? Me and you, two badass bitches running everything?"

"Like before."

"Exactly like before, only with a fresh start."

"I want that, too. I do, I do ..."

Before Mary could get more words out, Barbara interrupted. "But nothing can happen until I get that necklace back. It's real important to me. For sentimental reasons. I'm sure you understand."

"It's at home. I can put my hands on it in two minutes."

"Here. A show of good faith." Barbara reached under Tommy Logan's shirt, unhooked the money belt, and tossed it in the dirt at Mary's feet. "That's a lot of money right there. Take it. It's yours."

"Ain't this special." Tommy's voice was thin and weak. "Two gal pals sparking on one another again. I'm so touched I could take a piss."

Barbara kept her eyes locked on Mary. "The second thing, I need you to quit pointing that gun at me. It's looking right at me, the eye of the devil. Put it down, sugar."

"Okay. But—but—how do I know you won't shoot me?"

"I'm giving my word. I brought cigars."

"What about him?" Mary indicated Tommy Logan. "How do I know you're not still working with him?"

"I shot him, didn't I? Ain't a bullet worth something?"

Logan piped up. "Yeah, what're you gonna do about me, Doll?"

Barbara reached her gun hand around, pressed the barrel to Logan's chest and fired. His body hit the ground hard and never moved again.

"Two bullets. That convince you?"

Barbara didn't bother looking at Logan. Death has no imagination. It has one dimension, one look, and she'd seen it before.

She extended her arms with the gun pointed at Mary, just as Mary's gun was pointed at her. They stood no more than eight feet apart, the short space between them pulsing with longing and fear.

They waited, not breathing. A trucker's horn bellowed out on Fifty-First Avenue, and in the sullen quiet of the aftermath, they heard the first sounds of a vehicle approaching down the driveway.

"That's Fat Frankie. He doesn't know it yet, but he's going to help me take care of the bodies."

"I gotta get back to La Posada to round out my alibi. Whatta you say, can we put these guns down and go about our business?"

Barbara moved first, slowly lowering her gun arm until it was by her side. She stood that way, waiting, a wide-open target.

Mary, unblinking, didn't move. The gun stayed steady. Barbara watched Mary's eyes. They slowly emptied. Her stare crept on a spider's legs through Barbara's gut, and she thought she'd made a deadly mistake.

"Remember that first night, sugar? Me and you? I sure do."

Mary was a statue.

"That was like being born all over again. Like nothing I ever felt before. I know you felt it, too. Didn't you feel it, sugar?"

Barbara's words calmed Mary and brought her mind back.

"It was good, wasn't it, Barb?"

"No, it was great. Magical."

"Like a fur coat."

"Better than a fur coat."

"Better than a fur coat."

A heavy moment crawled by in the dangerous darkness by the canal.

"Know what I did, Barb? You'll never guess."

"What?"

"Made an appointment with Dr. Sergio. Thanks for the contact."

"There's my girl. We're on our way. Belmont Construction's gonna take off like crazy. Our lives will change, I promise you."

"That's what I want."

Inch by inch, Mary relaxed, lowering her arms and rising from a crouch. "Okay." She exhaled and motioned at Logan's body. "This one and his partner in the bushes, I know a place."

"Nobody can ever find them."

"The old Swilling Mine in the Superstitions."

"It's gotta be remote. I mean lost, gone, and bye-bye."

"It's way out there. They'll be living with the rattlesnakes until the last day."

"The guns. I'm sure Jimmy had one, too. Ditch them in the mountains."

"Easy, no problem."

"The necklace. I'll be at your house later to get it. We'll smoke a Cuban."

"Oh, Barb. I love the sound of that. I'm so happy."

CHAPTER THIRTY-THREE

Frankie Santiago pulled up in a black Ford F-150 pickup. Big tires and he had it jacked up. The engine sounded like a roaring lion. He stepped out wearing beige slacks and an untucked button-up red shirt with white stars on it.

"Good evening, Mary." Standing beside the Prius, he pulled up his pant legs and looked down. "Wore socks and everything. Clean, too, *más o menos.*"

Mary caught a powerful whiff of cologne. It made her gag. Did you put it on with a paintbrush?

"I said nothing about cologne."

"Tonight's supposed to be special, right? You had me do all this other stuff, wash my clothes and that. What's wrong with cologne?"

"I like it when men do exactly as I say."

"You're particular, that's for sure. Not that I mind, but this is some location you've found out here." He was smiling as he walked toward her. "Passed a red car on the way in. What was that about?"

"Change in plans, Frankie."

Fixated on Mary, he didn't notice Tommy Logan's body lying in the dirt, practically at his feet.

"I need help moving some cargo." She indicated the body.

Frankie glanced down and saw Logan on his back with a hole in his chest. Startled, he jerked back a few steps, almost falling down.

"What the hell? What the hell? Who is this?" Pointing: "Is he dead?"

"Extremely."

"What—what happened?"

"We'll be taking a drive. Your pickup works perfectly."

"Where? What the hell's going on?"

"Tonto National Forest. We need to get busy loading him up."

"In my truck? Are you nuts? I'm not doing that. This is a dead body. Uh-uh, sorry. No way. This man is dead, Mary."

When she stepped closer, Frankie saw the gun in her hand.

"Jesus, what—Mary, for crying out loud, this doesn't make sense. What's going on? Did you shoot this guy?"

"There's another one in the bushes. Sad, sad story. They traveled a long way and met the wrong women." Mary's face showed sudden surprise. "I believe I just wrote a country song. Do you like country music?"

Frankie held his hands straight out and shook his head like he was trying to clear it of buzzing bees. "I'm not—this—you—you can't be serious, Mary. This is way out of my league. I'm a legitimate businessman."

"That's one thing you're definitely not."

"A little money here and there, yeah, fine. But bodies? Dead guys? I can't be involved with stuff like this. No way, no way."

"I know how you paid for your fun house in Cave Creek."

Frankie's face turned to granite. "I don't know what you're talking about."

"Got two words for you. Chino Carrasco. Recognize that name?"

The granite cracked to pieces. Frankie sputtered, trying to speak, but nothing intelligible came out.

"Don't make me tell Chino you've been skimming."

"Mary, Mary, Mary."

"He'd love to know you paid for that house with his money."

"Oh, Jesus. Oh, Jesus. Mary. Don't, don't, don't. Chino will bury me."

"Burying's the easy part."

"Please, please, no, please."

"It's what he does before he buries you, that's what you should worry about. It won't be quick, Frankie. Chino will take his time. Piece by piece."

"Oh, God. Mary, Mary. Chino's a monster. Mary, don't. Jeremy, Eduardo, and Rogelio."

"What?"

"My kids. I got three kids. My whole world—you can't." He looked around at the darkness behind the warehouses as if searching for a way out. But there was no way out and nothing to say.

He ran his palms up and down his thighs to dry them. "Okay, anything, anything, anything. Just not Chino. Please."

Mary got the plastic drop cloths out of the Prius. She spread them out on the ground beside the car. Mary led Frankie into the bushes to Jimmy's body and Frankie dragged him by his ankles to the car.

He rolled the body onto one of the plastic sections and did the same with Logan. Frankie poured sweat. He looked like he'd just stepped out of the shower. He made small whimpering sounds as he worked.

Mary got some rope out of the Prius and cut it into lengths, and together they wrapped the plastic around the bodies and tied the ropes together, three lengths for each one.

Frankie backed his truck up and dropped the bodies into the bed. At Mary's instruction, he covered them with a blanket, placed a ladder atop the blanket, and secured it to the bodies with more rope.

He did as ordered and didn't say a word, except to mumble the Lord's Prayer and bless himself. Mary got her tequila bottle out of her pocket and, sipping, explained how it was going to go.

Frankie would drive the pickup to a Skoal and sawdust bar near Tempe. Dave's Roundup was set in a grubby strip mall near an entrance ramp to US Highway 60. Mary would follow in the Prius, jump into Frankie's pickup, and together they'd drive into the Tonto National Forest.

"No bright ideas, Frankie. Am I clear?"

"No ideas."

"You think of calling the cops or pulling a move, my partner gives Chino a ring-a-ling."

"I'm with you, Mary. All the way."

"I want you to step on it but keep to the speed limit. I don't want any conversations with cops. I'll be right behind you all the way. Do everything I tell you to do. Every single thing or you're dead."

"Jeremy, Eduardo, and Rogelio."

"Heard you the first time."

"They're grown now, doing real good. The youngest, he's away at college. Do you know what his GPA is?"

Mary disappeared inside herself. Years vanished and she saw scenes and people from Winchester College. "I like reading poetry. Like to write it, too. Used to. Wrote all the time. Before."

"Poetry. I never read no poetry."

"Sometimes life comes at you hard and it's too much."

"I'd say you're pretty far gone from poetry."

"Just start the fucking truck."

CHAPTER THIRTY-FOUR

They drove back to the 10 and down through the Valley toward Tempe and Dave's Roundup. From there, they got on Highway 60 and drove east. The traffic thickened around Apache Junction, but when they crossed the Tonto Forest boundary, the oncoming headlights became sporadic.

Mary's neck stiffened as she listened to Frankie's ragged breathing. "You're getting on my nerves."

"What am I doing?"

"Breathing."

"Like I can help it. I gotta breathe."

"You're not running a marathon. Act like a man and drive the stupid truck."

After Highway 60, they followed State Highway 88 north. South of Canyon Lake, Mary broke apart her burner phone and tossed it out the window and ordered Frankie to turn onto a two-track she remembered from her hiking days.

The road led up into the Superstitions. It started out hard-packed and easy and got rougher as they went. All the better, Mary thought.

She sipped her drink. They were nowhere now, high up in the wild country. Shining stars showed the way, backlighting the giant saguaros against the black sky. They looked like men watching from the hilltops.

The road at one time had been a railroad line for hauling ore. It climbed all the way, the truck bouncing and diving with every bump. Mary disassembled the two handguns and tossed the pieces out the window as they went.

At the seven-mile mark, the road became a foot trail, then a rabbit trail, and then boulders blocked their path and they could go no farther.

They walked the last stretch to a rock-strewn hill. An ore car lay on its side at the bottom, along with a litter of twisted metal and splintered wood from the headframe of the Swilling Mine, all of it surrounded by a three-strand barbed-wire fence.

Mary told Frankie to position the truck so that its high beams pointed up the hill. "That's where you're taking them."

"You think I can carry that deadweight all the way up that hill?"

"Aren't you a big, strong man, Frankie? That's what I like about you."

"You like me, huh? You got a funny way of showing it." He studied the hill and looked back at the truck. "Yeah, I can do it. Course I can do it."

"The night's getting long, Frankie. What're you waiting for?"

"What's up there?"

"Nothing but a hole in the ground."

"Deep?"

"Deep enough. A lot of men got rich scratching at this ground. Gold. It makes people go nuts. They say it gives you a fever."

They stood for a moment amid the silence of the mountains, staring up the hill. The memory of the day's brutal sun made the night sizzle.

"Anyway, that's where you're going, Frankie, up there. Drop the first one inside the fence and come back and get the other."

"You gonna help?"

"I'm going to watch."

"I don't need no help. It's just that, you know, I thought this was supposed to be a date."

"We are having a date. Only it's at your house. That's where I've been all night. With you up in Cave Creek. Get what I'm saying, Frankie?"

"Alibi."

"See, you're smart, too. You're going to tell the cops when they come around that I was with you at your pathetic sex palace all night."

"All night. Absolutely."

"Strong and smart, how could I lose? Get moving."

He hoisted the first body over his shoulder and dumped it over the barbed-wire fence onto the ground. He held the top wire down while he stepped over it with one leg, then the other, hoisted the body over his shoulder again, and trudged up the hill.

Mary leaned against the front of the truck, between the head-lights, the tequila bottle in one hand and the .380 in the other. She thought about how much she missed the outdoors.

With Frankie's strength ebbing, the second body proved harder. He stumbled on the trail, lost control, and the body rolled into a ditch. The plastic came loose and the head popped out, and Frankie saw the face staring up at him.

Dead eyes and bloodless lips stretched tight across two rows of nasty, used-up teeth.

"Ahhhh!" The fright hit him like a punch in the jaw. He landed flat on his back. His guttural scream echoed. He jumped to his feet and stared down at that horrible face.

"Scared, Frankie?"

"I ain't scared."

She laughed. He wiped his brow and went back to work, grunting as he hoisted the dead man over his shoulder and made his way slowly up the slope. He stumbled several more times and used his free hand on the ground to push himself upright and keep going.

At the top, he leaned forward to drop the body into the hole but missed. He set his feet and stiffened his back and picked the body up by the ankles and held it over the opening with two hands and let it go.

The dead man made sounds at first as he bumped against the sides of the shaft. Then the sounds stopped as he plunged farther and farther into the deep nothing.

Done with his work, chest heaving from the exertion, he got back to the truck and tried to catch his breath. He tugged at his shirt, fanning himself. "I'm soaking wet and wore out. But I did it. Told you I could do it."

They drove back to the highway in silence. As they neared the exit for Dave's Roundup, Frankie spoke up for the first time.

"Did you mean what you said earlier? About liking me, I mean?"

Mary didn't respond.

"I was thinking, you know, when all this blows over, maybe I could, ah, give you a call."

"If you call, text, or try to contact me in any way, I'll cut your throat."

He drove along quietly. "You know, most ladies, when they don't want to see a fellow, they just say no."

He exited the highway and pulled in next to the Prius in the Roundup parking lot.

"Where were we tonight, Frankie?"

"My place, all night long, having a great time." His chin hung on his chest. Exhausted, defeated, angry, his voice rising on each word: "And I did like you said, every little thing you said. Wore clean socks just for you. And cologne!"

Frankie was sick of the night and sick of what he was, and the only thing he could do about it was scream.

Mary paid no attention to his eruption. She sipped from the tequila bottle. Some of it leaked out and ran down her chin. She caught what she could with a lizard-like sweep of her tongue and wiped the rest away with her forearm.

"One more time, Frankie. You don't stick to the story, who do I call?"

"I'm not saying the name."

She jammed the gun into his ribs. "Say it."

"Go ahead and shoot. Do me a favor." His forehead plunked against the steering wheel.

"Poor man. Then I'll say it. Chino Carrasco."

"Jesus, Mary. I thought you were a nice girl."

"So did I. Good night, Frankie."

Mary got into the Prius and left.

CHAPTER THIRTY-FIVE

Driving away from the canal, Barbara swung into the first residential neighborhood she could find. She stopped in a darkened area and took off her Marilyn clothes and changed into her original outfit.

She'd worn a waist-length white shirt, two top buttons undone and a heart bellybutton chain visible along a thin strip of bare stomach. A pearl necklace filled the wide V at her neck. Her slacks were black, high-waisted, and wide-legged. The shoes were silver and had ankle straps and six-inch stiletto heels with a zipper up the back.

She used the overhead light and the rearview mirror to reapply her makeup and cover up Tommy Logan's handiwork.

Done with that and confident that she looked lovely, Barbara drove on to Paradise Valley and La Posada, a hacienda-style hilltop mansion surrounded by flaming torches.

The white stucco house had a long veranda and in front of that a pond with a bridge over it and hedge-maze gardens on both sides of the bridge. Light filled every window in all three stories, and the balconies buzzed with people drinking and talking, with more coming and going from every door.

Parking was in small lots behind the mansion, each separated from the big house by patches of desert accessible by winding driveways.

Barbara had her next moves planned out. She knew the parking lot she wanted. From there, she planned to enter the building through the delivery entrance. She couldn't risk going around to the front. Too many partygoers would see her returning.

Walking closer, Barbara saw two people standing outside the kitchen door. There was a man dressed in a chef's outfit and a girl who, by her outfit, looked to be a waitress. They were sharing a cigarette.

Not wanting close contact with anyone, Barbara waited behind a saguaro for them to finish their smoke and go back inside.

The minutes ticked off. Finishing off her alibi was critical to the plan.

Let's go. Let's go.

The chef took a last puff, dropped the cigarette, and stomped it with his foot.

That's it, that's enough. You've had your break. Now go back inside.

Instead, the chef stepped closer to the waitress. He towered over her. She looked up at him, big-eyed. By the turn of his head, Barbara could tell he was working her. He put his palm gently against her cheek. The waitress smiled and let her face fall into his palm.

They stayed that way, the chef whispering, until, with his free hand, he drew from his pocket a small mirror and a vial and held them in his palm for the girl to see. She covered her mouth and bounced on her toes in excitement.

He twisted the cap off the vial and sprinkled white powder onto the mirror. Using two hands, the girl held the mirror steady while the chef used a credit card to mark off lines. He snorted the drug using a rolled-up bill, then handed it to her and she did the same.

Barbara couldn't wait anymore and walked out of the darkness. The waitress saw her coming first and said something out of the corner of her mouth. The chef alerted and hid the mirror and the bill behind his back.

But they knew they'd been seen.

Saying nothing, Barbara tapped her nose and wiggled her fingers at the chef. He frowned, handed her the bill, and held the mirror out with two hands. Barbara leaned down and took two fast snorts. She sniffed and wiped her fanned fingers back and forth under her nose.

Barbara pointed at him. "What's your name, snowman?"

"I ain't no snowman." He tried to sound indignant, but it didn't come off.

"Plying this sweet little thing with coke, spitting game at her? Yeah, you're a snowman all right. Gimme another bump."

He held the mirror and Barbara took a long snort. "Name. I want it now."

"Diego."

"Diego. Not exactly original, is it?"

Barbara pointed to the girl. Her name was Maria. Nodding, Barbara stared and held it, eyes shifting from one to the other. The gap in power between the kitchen help and the beautiful guest didn't have to be stated. The stare expressed it perfectly.

When she had them where she wanted, Barbara motioned toward the delivery door. "I don't want to walk all the way around in these heels. You don't mind, I'll go in the back way."

The chef shrugged. "Sure, whatever."

"You didn't see me and I didn't see you two partaking of illicit narcotics out here in public. Disgraceful bullshit, the two of you. Honestly."

Not exactly sure what they'd encountered, they looked at each other and nodded.

"Diego and Maria. I got a good memory, but it'll be our secret."

Barbara held out the rolled-up bill. When the chef reached for it, she pulled it back, slipped it into her cleavage, and walked to the delivery door.

After the kitchen, she followed a hallway to the main room, where she grabbed a fluted drink off a waiter's tray as he passed by, and within minutes was part of the crowd again. She chatted, touched arms, and found everyone she met as beautiful and charming as ever.

The raspberry brie tartlets were outstanding.

Around midnight, she said her good-byes and drove to Mary's house, ditching Logan's gun, the Marilyn outfit, wig, and gloves in dumpsters along the way.

She got there after 1:00 a.m. Mary's Corolla was parked in the driveway as expected, the garage door closed. Barbara didn't have to check to know the Prius wasn't inside.

With the drive Mary had had ahead of her, deep into the Superstitions, it'd be a while until she returned. Parking on the street all that time was too risky, so she circled the neighborhood several times, listening to *My Fair Lady*.

She sang along. She could've danced all night.

At 2:45 a.m., she saw the blue Prius coming down the street. She rolled down the window and signaled with an arm wave. Going in the opposite direction, Mary pulled alongside.

"There you are, my love. What a drive. I felt like I was in the car forever. I thought about you the whole time, Barb. I missed you."

"What about the bodies?"

"Done. Frankie's shaking all over. He won't be a problem."

"And the necklace?"

"Did you miss me, too? I need to know."

Barbara got a strong whiff of tequila. Mary looked rattled. Desperate eyes. "Every minute, sugar."

"Let's go inside. I need to be near you. I need to hold you."

"Tonight's out of the question."

Mary's heart dropped. She pulled back, shocked. "Something's wrong. What's wrong? That's not what you said."

"Henry Belmont is dead in a motel room. There's a shitstorm coming and we have to be ready. We can't let up now or this whole thing will come apart."

"Just a few minutes, Barb. Please. Weren't we going to smoke a cigar?"

"Too risky."

Mary pleaded. She slurred her words. "I've been thinking about our first night. Like you said. I feel that way all over. Don't you? You said you did."

Barbara reached her hand out the window and Mary did the same. They held hands across the street. "Of course I do, sugar. We'll have plenty of nights ahead if we play this right. You get that, don't you?"

Mary's face darkened. She took a long time to answer. "I guess so, sure."

"The necklace."

"It's—yeah. Ah, like I said, it's inside."

"I'll park down here a ways and run in and grab it. What about Dorothy?"

"I gave her a sleeping pill before I left."

"Good, I'll be there in a sec."

Mary drove ahead. She pulled into the garage and closed the door.

Nothing added up right. Barbara had seemed so abrupt, so different. She reached up under her skirt and felt the .380 holstered against her thigh. She needed confirmation that it was there, needed to feel it against her hand.

Did I make a mistake at the canal? Did Barb play me?

No, no, no, no, no. She brought the cigars. She had the Cohibas ready.

She went to the back of the Prius, lifted the hatch, and took out her money sack. She emptied Tommy Logan's belt and put that cash in the sack, too, along with the belt.

She went inside, left the front door unlocked for Barbara, and walked down the hall to her bedroom. She pulled the bureau away from the wall, removed the false panel, opened the safe, and put the sack inside.

She sat on the edge of her bed with the cat in her lap.

"I know what you're thinking, Little Muffin, that you were right all along. But listen to me, listen. I'm giving Barb one last chance. I have to. I love her, and if she says she loves me, everything will be all right. If she doesn't, I'm ready. You have to trust me, Little Muffin, I'm ready for anything."

She cuddled the cat.

Outside, Barbara Belmont parked her SUV and stepped out. She felt the gathering wind and gazed at the dark sky. Another storm had rolled in. The wind beat at her, wet and relentless, and Barbara recognized it the same way you'd recognize a person.

Yes, she'd met this wind before, looked into its face, let its hot breath burn her skin, and knew nothing good would come from it.

She stood beside the open car door and didn't move. She thought about the look on Mary's face, her scarecrow eyes, the heavy smell of tequila and what it did to her, and that evil little .380 strapped to her leg.

Barbara took the Beretta out of her pocket, leaned into the SUV, and dropped it into the glove box. She fished Mary's Glock out from under the front seat and unscrewed the suppressor.

With the suppressor off, the gun fit easily at the small of her back. She glanced around at the silent street. At the run-down cars, the run-down houses, and thought about the lives of the people inside.

Nobody gives you anything. You get what you're willing to fight for, what you're willing to bleed for. If it comes to that, I'm ready.

She walked down the sidewalk to Mary's house.

CHAPTER THIRTY-SIX

Barbara Belmont passed through the front door as quietly as she could. The house was dark except for the square of light coming from Mary's bedroom. She walked down the hall and found Mary holding a screwdriver, her face ashen.

"Do you love me, Barb?"

"Of course I do. I don't even know why you're asking."

"Because I need to know."

"We haven't got time for this now."

"Time? We don't have time? Did you really just say that to me?"

"I need to get home and clean Henry's Beretta and put it back where it's supposed to be. In the morning my phone's gonna start ringing and there's going to be banging at my door. Cops. Asking questions. Yours, too. You remember Henry's dead, right?"

"You came back for the necklace. Not for me, the necklace."

"That was the deal."

"Yes, we had a deal, a transaction." That last word came out smoking hot.

"Didn't we work this out at the canal? I told you, everything's fine, better than fine. Girl, you've been the best thing to happen to me in a long time."

"You mean that? Me?"

"You. Mary Rose Cleary. How many times do I have to say it?"

"I've never been special to—anybody."

"Act two, me and you. You like poetry, don't you? Keep saying that little ditty to yourself and we'll be all right."

"Act two, me and you."

"There you go. Now, where's my necklace at?"

A folding chair stood against the wall near the bathroom. Mary opened it, set it against the wall underneath a cooler vent. "Dorothy can't get up here."

She climbed onto the chair and reached up to unscrew the vent cover. She couldn't get high enough to get a good angle on the screws, lost her grip on the screwdriver, and it fell to the floor. When Barbara bent over to pick it up, Mary saw the Glock pressed against her back.

"That's my gun. Wait, wait, wait—you said you ditched it."

"I will. I just haven't yet."

"That's not what you said." Mary's voice shook with mounting panic. "You said you'd gotten rid of it. But you kept it. You lied to me. Why'd you keep it?"

"I'm gonna get rid of it, I promise. You need to calm down."

"Don't tell me to calm down. You brought it into my house. Why'd you bring that gun into my house?"

"I don't know, I just did."

Barbara had no good answer. She couldn't say the truth, that the gun offered insurance in case something happened, that she didn't want to use it, never intended to use it, but needed it anyway, because that was how she lived.

By watching out for herself, by measuring angles, by always following her instincts. All her life, every day of her life starting as a little girl, that was what she did best. It was her gift, the reason she was still alive.

She always listened to the wind and did exactly what it told her.

"To use it on me? Is that why you kept the gun? To set me up for Henry? To steal my money and take back your necklace? Is that your plan?"

"Don't, don't. I'm telling you, no. I swear to you, no. Isn't that enough?"

Mary's face blazed red. "You betrayed me again!"

Standing on the chair, Mary jerked up her skirt to reach for the .380. Her practice sessions had paid off. She got the gun out swiftly and with ease.

"No! This isn't what I want!" But it was too late. Barbara had no choice, and no time to go for the Glock.

She kicked the chair over. Mary toppled to the floor, the .380 bouncing away. They wrestled. Flat on her back, Mary socked Barbara in the jaw. Her eyes blurred. The colored lights made it New Year's Eve in August.

Mary reached around Barbara's back for the Glock. But Barbara recovered her senses and grabbed her hand. On her knees, straddling, she pinned Mary's wrists to the floor and leaned down close, almost mouth to mouth.

Screaming: "Will you listen to me!? It's not like you think!"

"Liar!"

Mary kicked and fought with everything she had. Her breath blew out in gusts and groans. Rage made her strong. She freed her right hand and got hold of the Glock. Barbara gripped her wrist with two hands, raised her knee and slammed Mary's arm against it.

The gun fell to the carpet. They grappled for it. Mary got to it first, but Barbara was right behind her. She covered Mary's hand with hers but couldn't shake the gun loose, and that left her one option, one chance to stay alive.

Using all her strength, she forced the barrel against Mary's right temple, covered Mary's trigger finger with hers, and squeezed.

A deep silence followed the blast. Blood spilled across the carpet. Barbara sat on her heels, her face sweaty. She stayed that way, staring at nothing, thinking nothing.

When she caught her breath, she went to the bathroom and washed the blood spatter off her hands. From the vanity under the sink, she got a pair of rubber gloves and put them on.

She stepped onto the chair and removed the screws on the vent cover. Not tall enough to see inside, she stretched onto her toes, reached in, and felt around. The necklace was there. She put it in her pocket. She screwed the vent cover on and stepped down.

Now she had to do something about the guns.

She picked up the .380, raised Mary's skirt, and slipped it into her thigh holster. She picked up the Glock, racked the slide back repeatedly to eject all thirteen rounds.

Back in the bathroom, she found a container of Clorox wipes. She carried the wipes and the Glock and the bullets onto the patio and shut the French doors to keep the smell of bleach out of the bedroom.

Barbara knew how to do this. She'd known in the aftermath of Ricky Peel's untimely death, too.

She wiped the bullets down one at a time to remove her prints. She wrapped a wipe over her gloved index finger and pressed it into the grooves at the bottom of the bullets to remove any DNA. She wiped the gun handle and the rear portion of the slide, careful to leave the blowback of Mary's blood and brains on the barrel.

She cleaned and reloaded the magazine and palmed it back into the well. She put the used wipe in her pocket and went back inside and got down on her heels next to Mary's body. She put the gun in Mary's right palm and pressed her dead fingers around it, paying special attention to her index finger on the trigger.

With that done, she put the gun on the carpet near Mary, thinking, Now I have what I need—blood spatter on Mary's right hand and on the gun, gunpowder residue on her hand, and the spent shell on the floor beside the body.

That shell would match the one from the motel. Barbara dug it out of her pocket, cleaned it off, swiped it against Mary's fingers and palm to collect DNA, and put it in Mary's pocket.

At the bathroom sink, she washed the gloves and dried them with a towel. Putting them back on, she dragged the bureau away from the wall. She used the birthday of the late Henry Belmont to open the safe and remove the money sack.

She put the necklace in the sack, along with the screwdriver and the gloves. She put the sack on the bed. In Mary's closet she found her Russian sable fur coat, put it on, and checked herself in the mirror. She adjusted the fit on her shoulders and toyed with the collar.

This coat was her favorite of the three. She loved the way she looked in it. Her hair was a mess from the struggle. She used her hands to brush it into place as best she could.

Heading toward the door, she stopped beside Mary's lifeless body, touched two fingertips to her lips, kissed them, and pressed those fingers against Mary's cold lips. She grabbed the sack off the bed and walked down the hall.

She'd heard no sound and thought she was alone, until a tremendous boom shattered the silence of the house. The gunshot, so powerful, so loud in the closed space, made the walls shake, after which came Dorothy's high, screeching voice.

"Halt! Halt, or I'll shoot you dead!"

All Dorothy could see was a figure coming toward her along the darkened hallway. Wearing that billowy fur coat, Barbara looked huge, like one of the monsters that so troubled Dorothy's sleep. The sight frightened her, and she was gripping that Civil War pistol. She held it up, ready to fire again.

"Whoa, whoa, what the hell!" Barbara stopped in midstep with her hands up. "What the hell are you doing!? Dorothy!"

"Halt! I mean it! I'll shoot you down!"

"Dorothy, it's me. It's Barbara Belmont."

"Who?" Dorothy strained to see.

"Barbara Belmont, Mary's friend. You could've killed me."

"Barbara?" She cocked her head and squinted.

"Yes, Barbara. Barbara Belmont. Now, I'm gonna step into the living room and turn on a goddammed light. Jesus."

"You don't have to use that language."

"That's what you're worried about right now? My language? You almost killed me. Don't shoot, Dorothy." She found a lamp and flipped the switch.

Dorothy saw clearly that it was Barbara but still wouldn't lower the gun.

"It's me, okay. Remember? That night you were playing cards?"

"Was that a shot I heard earlier? I was asleep and heard a loud bang that sounded like it came from Mary's bedroom." The big revolver wavered in Dorothy's frail hands. She was weak and foggy from the sleeping pill Mary had given her.

"Easy with that thing. How about putting it down?"

"Answer my question."

"You're absolutely right it was a gunshot. But it was an accidental discharge. There's no problem here."

"Where's Mary at?"

"In the bedroom. She's fine."

Dorothy called to Mary and got no response.

"I'd really appreciate it if you put that thing down."

Dorothy called a second time. Dead silence. "Don't sound fine to me. Why ain't she answering me?"

"She's lying down."

Dorothy pointed to the bag over Barbara's shoulder. "What's that you got there? You stealing from us?"

Barbara showed her hands in a gesture of calm. "I'll show you. I'm going to reach into the bag real slow and show you. Just relax." Her hand came out holding a fistful of bills. Dorothy liked what she saw very much.

With great caution, Barbara stepped forward and handed the bills to Dorothy, whose raggedy old face came alive. The gun dropped into her lap, and with two hands she reached for the cash like a starving beggar.

"There's more where that came from, a lot more. You want some?"

"I sure do. Gosh."

"I'll wake up Mary. She'll tell you all about it."

In Mary's bedroom, Barbara pulled the gloves out of the sack and put them on again. She stepped around the bloodstain, picked up the Glock, and walked back to the living room with her left arm hanging straight down at her side and her index finger on the trigger.

Dorothy was exulting, embracing the bills, cooing over them. Barbara raised the Glock and fired a bullet into Dorothy's heart. She died instantly with the money in her hands and the pistol in her lap.

Barbara smiled and walked back to the bedroom.

She put the gun in Mary's right palm and pressed her fingers around it, as before, and placed the gun on the carpet. She put both gloves back in the sack and returned to Dorothy, who sat in her wheelchair the way she always had, only now with her mouth hanging open and her head bent onto her shoulder.

Barbara gathered the bills off her lap, the bloody ones, too, dropped them in the sack. Her mind was calm and clear as she thought about the setup.

The young, innocent, and loyal Mary Rose Cleary had used her Glock to murder her boss and lover, Henry Belmont, out of jealousy, her stepmother out of derangement, then, sadly, she took her own life. Perfect.

Barbara walked outside. On the sidewalk she stopped and pulled a cigar tube out of her pocket, removed the cigar, bit off the end, and spat it into a Clorox wipe. She put the wipe back in her pocket and rolled the Cohiba around on her tongue. She lit it and drew.

The taste and smell were magical. She looked back at the house.

"Too bad, Red, I thought we found it."

Wearing that fabulous fur, Barbara Belmont walked down the sidewalk puffing her Cuban. The storm had given up and moved on, taking the wind with it and leaving behind a cloudless black sky.

The sliver moon threw down small mercy, but Barbara kept to the shadows, lest some sleepless soul be alerted to the *click, click, click* of her stiletto heels.

ABOUT THE AUTHOR

Boston-born Leo W. Banks worked as a reporter for years, winning more than 38 statewide, national and international journalism awards. His first novel, *Double Wide*, won two Spur awards from the Western Writers of America -- for Best First Novel of 2018 and Best Western Contemporary Novel. *True West* magazine called it the Western crime novel of the year. The sequel, *Champagne Cowboys*, received a starred review from *Publishers Weekly*. He lives in Arizona.

Made in the USA
Las Vegas, NV
19 December 2024